Six Months in Montana

by

Pamela Kelley

SIX MONTHS IN MONTANA

By: Pamela Kelley

Published by Piping Plover Press

Copyright 2013, Piping Plover Press

All rights reserved.

Edited by Tessa Shapcott

Cover by Susan Coils

ISBN: 9780615932910

Author's Note

I am so excited that you are here! Thank you for coming and I hope you enjoy this story. I chose the setting of Montana after a very close friend decided to move there after visiting once and falling in love with it. She took a big risk moving to Bozeman, with no family and only one friend who lived hours away. But, it truly was meant to be as she quickly found a great job and shortly after joining a local kayak club, made a new friend who a year or so later became her husband. They welcomed their first baby a few months ago and so it seemed fitting that the fictional town of Beauville, which I set about 30 miles or so from Bozeman would be the setting for this romance.   ~Pam

Dedicated in loving memory to my mother, Marcia Merrick Ford, and my Grandfather, Kenneth L. Ford.

Chapter 1

"This is a joke right?" Christian Ford looked at his lawyer and best friend, Travis Jones, in disbelief. Now he understood why Travis had insisted that he come by his office for an official reading of his grandfather's will. "Are you seriously telling me that he changed his will less than a month before he died, and added this condition?"

"I'd love to tell you I'm kidding, but your grandfather was very clear about what he wanted." Travis added, "I tried to talk him out of it. Told him you haven't even seen her in years. But he was insistent, said he ran into her at the market last month. She was home for a quick visit, and they got to chatting."

"Doesn't she live in New York City now?" Christian hadn't seen, or thought of Molly in years.

"She does. Works for one of the large hotel chains. Sounds like she's done pretty well too."

"So this makes absolutely no sense then. Her life isn't here." Christian glanced around the office, not really seeing the varnished dark wood bookcases, or the view out of the window behind Travis, which overlooked Main Street in Beauville, Montana, a small town just outside Bozeman. Main Street served as the center of town, and most of its small shops and businesses were along this stretch.

"Your grandfather seemed to think she'd be better off here."

"It's absolutely ridiculous. She'll never agree to it. Why would she?"

Travis leaned back in his plush leather chair and picked up the will, shuffling the pages until he found the passage he was looking for.

"Well, you just have to stay married for six months. She'll be free to go after that if she wishes, and it might be worth her while."

"Have you called her yet?" Christian was having a hard time wrapping his head around this. His grandfather had always marched to his own drum and had had plenty of ideas about how Christian should do things, but he'd never meddled to this extreme before.

"I spoke with her briefly yesterday. She's on her way here, meeting us in an hour at Delancey's."

"We're not meeting here, in the office?" Delancey's was the best restaurant in the area.

"Given the situation, I thought the least we could do is buy her dinner."

***

Molly Bishop was tired and annoyed, though admittedly curious. It had already been a long day. She'd juggled her schedule a bit, going in to work earlier so she could duck out and catch a four o'clock flight. She made it, just barely, and it was an hour into the flight before she felt herself finally starting to relax. With the two-hour time difference between New York and Montana, she'd just about make it to dinner by seven. She'd also arranged for someone to fill in for her tomorrow and, truth be told, she could use this short break. Molly loved her job as assistant general manager at the Clarendon Hotel in Manhattan, but on a good day it was stressful, and lately there had been more fires than usual that had needed to be put out.

The hotel was an impressive one, but it was old and badly in need of renovating. In the past few months that had become painfully evident, as one major breakdown after another had needed attending to: the water heater had burst in the basement, creating a huge mess; two stoves in the kitchen had stopped working in the same week and, most damning of all, a famous reviewer had described the Clarendon online as 'old and drab, like a beautiful woman who is unfortunately showing her age'.

Molly thrived on the pace and excitement of running a top hotel in New York City. The energy there was like nowhere else. Things were always happening, and she was right in the middle of it, making sure that everyone who stayed at The Clarendon was well taken care of. That was noted in the same critical review: 'Though the hotel is desperately in need of a face lift, their standard of service remains as excellent as ever'.

Molly put a copy of the review in her scrapbook and had high hopes for her own career review next week. She was overdue for a promotion to general manager, the dream job she had been working toward for years, and it felt like it was finally about to happen. Obviously, it couldn't take place unless there was an opening for her to move into, but the current GM had been with the organization for seven years, a long time in the hotel world, and Molly hadn't been able to help but notice that Paul had recently been in several hush-hush meetings with the hotel's owners. Change was definitely in the air.

When the plane landed and Molly stepped outside, she immediately felt the sense of peace that always swept over her when she returned to Montana. As much as she loved New York, Montana still felt like home. The air here always had a calming effect on her. She tensed up a bit though, as she got into her rental car and started driving toward Beauville. Travis hadn't said much on the phone, just that there was something in Christian Ford's grandfather's will that concerned her, and that they should meet immediately to discuss it.

She couldn't imagine why Christian's grandfather had thought to include her in his will. When she'd run into him last month at the grocery store, it had been the first time she'd seen him in almost ten years. Once they'd got to talking though, the years had fallen away, and it seemed like only yesterday that she and Christian had been next door neighbors and best friends. They'd even shared a dog. Toby had been a stray that showed up one day and stayed, going back and forth between Molly's house and Christian's. When Molly was just fourteen, her father had died suddenly of a heart attack, and although Uncle Richard, her father's brother, lived in Beauville, her mother had had no other family in the area. They'd moved to New York two months later, to Brooklyn, where her Aunt Betty lived, and it had been decided that Toby would stay with Christian. Once a dog had enjoyed all that Montana could offer, how could he live in the city? It had made perfect sense at the time…But now Molly saw dogs everywhere she went in Manhattan.

Molly pulled into Delancey's parking lot at a few minutes before seven. It looked like they were doing a good business for a Wednesday night. Delancey's was one of only three restaurants in town and was without question the best. They were known for steak and Molly's stomach rumbled at the thought of it. She'd missed lunch and hadn't eaten on the plane, except for a small bag of pretzels.

She grabbed her purse and headed into the restaurant. Travis and Christian were already seated at a corner table and waved her over. She recognized Travis immediately, as she'd seen him briefly the last time she was in town. Both her mother and Aunt

Betty were living here now. They'd come to visit one of her mother's friends a few years ago, and after just minutes in Montana, Aunt Betty had fallen in love and easily talked her mother into moving back to the area. Aunt Betty loved to entertain and half the town was at her most recent party, including Travis.

Both men stood when Molly reached the table, and Christian pulled out a chair for her. He held out his hand and said, "Thanks for coming." Molly shook both of their hands before settling into her seat. She was surprised that Christian seemed a little nervous. It had been many years since she'd seen him, and he'd grown into an impressive looking man. He smiled and she caught her breath. He still had the cutest dimples, and when he smiled the effect was devastating. Molly had heard that he'd done very well running his grandfather's business and, over the years, had expanded, so that now he had almost fifty men working for him. She must have imagined that he looked nervous.

"Christian, I am so sorry for your loss. Your grandfather was a special man."

"Thank you." They made small talk for a few minutes, as the waiter brought Molly a glass of Cabernet and then they put their orders in. The wine was excellent, rich and smooth, and she'd just taken another sip when Travis got down to business.

"I figured we might as well get this out of the way first, then we can relax and enjoy our steaks." It seemed as though he was trying to make light of something, which Molly found odd. She'd thought it was sweet that Mr. Ford had thought to include her in his will. It had been wonderful to bump into him last month; he'd been as feisty as ever, even though it had also been clear that he had slowed down quite a bit. Still, Molly never would have guessed that he'd been sick. He'd been ninety-four when he'd died, and had lived well right up until the end, when he'd gone to bed one night and never woken up. She was more than surprised she featured in his will, and imagined he'd left her a small token to remember him by, maybe one of his crystal animals. He'd had quite a collection and Molly had always admired them as a child.

"As I mentioned on the phone, Mr. Ford thought very highly of you." Travis paused for a moment, glancing at Christian, before turning his attention back to Molly and clearing his throat before continuing. His voice was a little shaky as he continued— Molly had never seen him so flustered. Travis was always so cool and collected. This wasn't like him at all.

"Yes, so as I was saying, Mr. Ford liked you, quite a bit actually. So much so that he thought it would be a very good idea for you to marry Christian."

Molly almost spat out her wine. "What?" By the look on Christian's face, he didn't look too happy about the idea either. "I don't understand."

"After Mr. Ford ran into you, he stopped by my office the next day and added a provision to his will, a condition under which Christian will only inherit the Ford ranch if the two of you get married immediately."

Molly was speechless. No wonder Travis was a little flustered. If he didn't look so uncomfortable, she'd wonder if he was joking, but it was obvious that he was quite serious.

"This is ridiculous. Why would he do this?"

Travis looked at Christian, who then explained, "My grandfather approved of almost everything I've done, except when it came to dating. I haven't really been serious about anyone in years, and he wasn't thrilled about the ones I have dated. He'd been after me for a long time to settle down. I told him that you can't rush these things, but truthfully I have no interest in getting married and he knew it."

"Okay, but why me? No offense, but why on earth would I agree to this? You both know I live and work in Manhattan. My life isn't here."

"He always liked you, and knew we used to get along."

"We were just kids." Molly protested.

Travis jumped in to further explain, "It's really not that bad. You just have to stay married for six months. If you both want out after that, there's no problem."

"Yes, but even if I were open to doing this, I couldn't. I have a job and an apartment clear across the country. Unless a long-distance marriage would be okay?" It was a lame attempt at humor on her part, a way to lighten the mood. The whole thing was too surreal.

"No, that wouldn't work." Travis pulled the will from a manila folder and flipped to the last page, where the terms of this arrangement were apparently detailed. "According to his instructions, you need to marry within the month, and live together as husband and wife for at least six months after that."

"He was quite the matchmaker. This is obviously not at all what I expected. I was thinking, maybe, one of his little crystals to remember him by."

"I know this is a lot to take in," Travis sympathized.

"It's flattering that he thought so highly of me, but it's a bit puzzling too. Honestly, you don't expect me to really do this? I'm sorry, but it just doesn't make sense for me. I'm not in a position to put my life on hold for the next six months."

"I understand," Christian said. "I don't blame you at all."

The waiter arrived with their steaks, and Christian immediately cut into his and started eating. Travis didn't.

"There's more to this. What you decide to do could affect others."

Molly's steak was delicious, but this remark caused her to put her fork down and pay closer attention, as Travis continued.

"The Ford Ranch employs nearly sixty men, all locals, most of whom have families here. I believe your Uncle Richard is among them. There is a sizable bank account that goes with the ranch and there's money there for operating costs, payroll and other emergencies. But if Christian doesn't inherit the ranch, he won't have access to the bank account and no way to meet payroll."

"That's awful!" But something didn't add up here, Molly was under the impression that Christian was a wealthy man. She was about to ask about this, when Christian spoke up, almost as if he knew what she was thinking.

"Almost all of my money is tied up in the ranch." He explained. "Just this past year, I took out a personal line of credit to expand and improve the main house, where I live. I'm maxed out."

"But surely the business has a line of credit?" Molly asked. The look on Christian's face tugged at her emotions and her first instinct was to help, but how could she? It was really too much to take in.

"The bank won't approve releasing additional funds until the matter of ownership is made clear. And there is a potential buyer." Christian added in a clipped tone.

"That would be a last resort." Travis explained. "This buyer is known for buying ranches at a deep discount, cutting costs drastically by laying off up to fifty per cent of staff and then reselling a year or two later at a huge profit." He paused for effect before adding, "I don't think I have to tell you that would decimate our town."

"Why would your grandfather do this to you? To the town?" Molly's memories of Mr. Ford didn't include someone who was this manipulative.

"He always boasted about being a good judge of character. I think he was counting on you to say yes." Christian looked serious as he added, "You don't have to, though. None of this is your fault. It's not fair that my grandfather expected us to do this, especially you."

"It's a lot to take in." Molly agreed, and half-heartedly cut into her steak. She'd been so hungry when she arrived here, but now her appetite had vanished.

"I think he meant well; he was a romantic at heart." Travis said with a smile, obviously trying to lighten the mood.

"Tell her about the Rose Cottage." Christian shot a look at Travis

"Right, of course. Mr. Ford didn't expect you to give up everything and get nothing in return. For your trouble, he wanted to compensate you with a piece of land and a house that has been in the family for years. It needs a bit of work, but the location and potential are there."

"Isn't that…" Molly began, and Christian jumped in to finish, "Yes, it's where my grandfather first lived, when he and my grandmother moved here. They lived there for years, until my grandmother died, about ten years ago. He moved in with me then, at the main house, to be closer to everyone. He said Rose

Cottage was too big for one person, but I think he just didn't want to be alone. I enjoyed his company." His voice broke a bit, and Molly's first instinct was to reach out and touch his hand. But before she could do that, he'd already pulled himself together and was cutting into his steak again.

"When do you need an answer by?" Molly asked. She needed to process this. It was a big decision, and one that would affect other people.

Travis brightened at this, possibly sensing that Molly might have a hard time saying no. "We can give you a week. We'll need to update the bank on ownership status by then and give an answer to our potential buyer."

Molly took a final bite of steak and chewed thoroughly before saying anything.

"I honestly don't know what I am going to do." She looked at both of them. "I'm up for a big promotion, the job I've always wanted. It's a lot to give up."

"Just think about it," Travis said, while Christian signaled the waiter for the check.

"Thank you for coming, and for listening." Travis added. "I assume we'll see you at the funeral tomorrow?"

"Of course. I'll be there."

Molly drove straight to her mother's house after dinner. Her Aunt Betty and mother were relaxing in the den, sipping a glass of wine and watching the latest episode of The Bachelorette. The two of them were debating whether or not the remaining bachelors were really 'in it for love', or not.

"Molly is that you?" her mother called out as Molly let herself in. "We're in here. Pour yourself a glass of Merlot and join us."

Molly did just that and, since she knew they were dying of curiosity, she filled them in on Christian's 'proposal'. When she'd finished delivering the details, the response she got was not what she expected: absolute silence. After a few long minutes, her mother finally spoke first. "I honestly don't know what to say. I've never heard of such a thing, not in this day and age anyway. Of course you said no, right? You're about to get that promotion you've always wanted, and worked so hard for. Plus, you love New York, right?" Her mother sounded both defiant and wistful at the same time, and Molly knew she'd love to have her living back close to both of them again.

"Well, I think it sounds like a dream come true!" Aunt Betty exclaimed. "Christian's gorgeous, and it's not like you won't be paid well for the inconvenience. Plus, maybe the old man was right; what if you fall in love? It could happen."

"Neither one of us is looking to fall in love." Molly corrected. "Not with each other anyway. I mean, I'd love to find Mr. Right someday, but my life is in Manhattan, and Christian made it very clear that he has no interest in marriage, to anyone."

"So, what are you going to do?" Her mother asked quietly.

"I have no idea. I have a week to decide."

"Well, try not to think about it, and just go with your gut, do what feels right." Aunt Betty said, and then couldn't help adding, "But remember, we'd love to have you living nearby again!"

The next few days flew by but, by Wednesday, Molly still hadn't decided what to do. As she stepped out of her apartment to head to work, she caught her breath at the beauty of the city. The trees along her street were always dressed in a smattering of delicate tiny white lights, and it was still dark enough outside that they were lit and casting a cheery glow on the neighborhood. There was a magical feeling in the air and Molly felt a bit excited for the first time all week. Today was the day of her review and she would hopefully find out about that promotion.

Chapter 2

The hotel was booked solid, due to one of the many conventions in town, and Molly didn't stop all day, until finally, just before five, Ben Peterson, the General Manager, found her.

"Molly, are you ready to meet? Let's go into the Vincent room." The small meeting room was right around the corner from where they stood. It would be more convenient than heading all the way down to the first floor and his office, where they'd be more likely to be interrupted.

Once they were settled, Ben jumped right in and gave her another glowing annual review, then finished with the good news she'd been hoping for.

"So, we were intending to reward you with a promotion to GM. The original plan was for me to move to the group's newest hotel, get that up and running, and for you to move into my slot here." He was beaming and Molly smiled back; this was exactly what she'd hoped for. Yet, she wasn't feeling as excited as she'd imagined she would. Because she knew what her decision had to be. Six months wasn't a long time; she could always come back and keep working towards the GM role.

"But last month, things changed." The smile left Ben's face, and Molly snapped to attention, wondering if she'd heard right.

"The hotel was sold last month, and they want me to stay on here to ensure a smooth transition to the new ownership. It's not all bad; the organization still wants to promote you. But it has to be delayed a bit, probably by a year or so, until the dust settles here."

Molly felt oddly numb, and relieved. Nothing was going to change here, not anytime soon. Six months away wouldn't make any difference, after all.

"The good news though, is that the new owners want to do a major renovation right away to restore the Clarendon to her former beauty. So, by the time you take over, she'll be like a sparkly new hotel, and all yours."

Molly spoke up then, feeling secure in her decision, though she knew what she was about to say would come as a complete surprise.

"Ben, I really do appreciate this opportunity, and everything that I've been able to experience here. I need to take a leave of absence though, if that's possible? I'll understand if it's not. I have a family situation, a personal matter in Montana that I need to attend to for the next few months. I will help as much as I can to get someone else up to speed."

Ben looked shocked, "I hope everything is okay?" He spoke cautiously, and Molly knew he was thinking the worst.

"No one is sick. It's nothing like that. It's just too complicated to explain. Like I said, I will totally understand if a leave of absence isn't possible, but I hope it is. I really love working here."

"No promises, but I'll see what I can work out for you."

As Molly was gathering up her things to leave for the day, she thought how funny it was that once her decision had been made, the rest of the pieces had seemed to fall together. She'd only just left her meeting with Ben, when she'd run into several of her colleagues in the employee break room. Stephanie, one of the front desk receptionists, had been in the middle of telling Jane, who also worked the front desk, that her roommate had just informed her that her boyfriend was going to move in, and if she wanted to find another place to live, that would be ok.

"It wasn't very subtle. But what am I going to do? I can pay rent on a small apartment, but I don't have enough saved to cover first, last and security; that's a fortune. Plus I don't have any things of my own. I'd have to find a furnished place. I could rent another room, I suppose, but I would really love to have my own place, and no roommates."

Molly had worked with Stephanie for several years, and knew her to be reliable and hard-working and, overall, a genuinely nice person. She hadn't hesitated a second before offering up her apartment as a sublet.

"It'll be for about six months at least, maybe a little longer, and available the first of the month." Stephanie, knowing how hard good apartments were to come by, had gratefully agreed on the spot.

Molly made her way home slowly, amazed and relieved that she'd made this crazy decision, and that she'd found someone to sublet her place so quickly. The long day had caught up to her, and she was looking forward to a small glass of wine and a bowl of pasta with her favorite creamy sauce. She'd discovered it by accident one day, when she'd dropped a spoonful of hummus onto her pasta and then was pleasantly surprised to learn that, when mixed with a bit of the pasta cooking water, it made an insanely delicious sauce.

It was almost seven by the time she reached her building, a pretty old townhouse in a decent neighborhood at the beginning of the Upper East Side. It was starting to get dark, and Molly couldn't quite place who the tall man was standing outside the entrance, but something about him seemed familiar. As she got closer, he waved and smiled and she stopped in her tracks. Christian Ford was waiting outside her building.

"What are you doing here?"

"Well, hello to you, too."

"I'm sorry, I was just surprised to see you here of all places."

"Well, since you came to us, I thought it only fair that I come to you and make my appeal." Was she imagining it or did he sound a little nervous?

"What are you talking about? I can't believe you are here."

Christian shoved his hands further into his long coat and exhaled slowly. He looked tired and cold, and Molly wondered how long he'd been waiting for her.

"Are you going to invite me in? It might be a little more comfortable inside and this could take a few minutes to explain well."

"Of course, come in." Molly felt a bit flustered as she dug out her key to let them into the building, and then they walked up silently to her third floor apartment. She opened the door and he followed her in.

Like most New York City apartments, her place was quite small. Molly had never minded though; it had everything she needed. There was a cozy bedroom, compact bathroom and a decent sized living room with exposed brick. There was also a gas fireplace, which Molly always turned on when there was even the slightest chill in the air. Just looking at the shimmering glow of the fire always warmed and cheered her up. The kitchen was one of those tiny, galley-sized ones, just the bare basics, but it opened into the living room and that gave the illusion of more space. For one person, it was perfect.

"Can I offer you a drink? I have a bottle of wine open."

"If it's not too much trouble I'd love a glass, but only if you're joining me."

"Of course, I'm ready for one." Molly shot him a smile, and then poured both of them a glass of Cabernet and set them down on the breakfast bar that separated the kitchen and living room. There were two bar stools there and it was Molly's favorite spot to eat when she was home, even though she had a cute little table in a corner of the living room. She and Christian settled onto the bar stools, and then Christian started talking.

"So, I have an idea I wanted to run by you, if you decide to take us up on this crazy offer. I know you are giving up a lot, and you mentioned that you have big promotion coming at work. But I was thinking, I'm sure you're amazing at what you do, or they wouldn't even be considering you for such a big job. You could pick up where you left off in six months or so. This might slow you down a little, but maybe not."

Molly raised her eyebrows at this. How could taking six months off possibly not slow her down? Although, given the actual situation, with the delay of her promotion, it probably wouldn't have much of an effect. But, Christian had no way of knowing that.

"You know Rose Cottage, which Travis mentioned?" he asked, and Molly nodded. "Well, it's big, really big; certainly it was too big for Gramps, which was the main reason he moved in with me. But it's really a large house, with six bedrooms and a few extra rooms that could be converted into bedrooms. It would need a little remodeling to get there, but it could be a great little inn or bed and breakfast—you know the type of place I'm talking about. There's a real need in the area for something like that. Beauville and Bozeman have been growing like gangbusters over the past five years. I could arrange for the muscle to make it look pretty, if you wanted to run it. Could be a heck of a fun project for you, maybe even a way to fill out your resume." In his excitement, Christian's leg bumped into hers and she felt a charge of energy that was unexpected. She quickly moved her leg away, and then realized that Christian had stopped talking and was waiting for her reaction. He'd looked so much younger than his age as he'd been talking, and it was clear that he was hoping and needing Molly to agree. She decided to end his anxiety.

"That sounds really great, and just so you know, I already gave my notice earlier today. I've decided to do this. It feels like the right thing to do, and if I'm being honest, I could use the break and would love to spend some time with Mom and Aunt Betty.

Christian set his wine glass down and grinned. His relief was obvious.

"So, it's decided then. I can't tell you how much this means to me and to all of my men."

"Cheers!" Molly raised her glass and then tapped it against his.

"How long are you in town for?" She asked. Christian glanced at his watch suddenly before answering.

"Not long. In fact, I have to run and catch a cab to the airport. I'm on a flight back in a few hours. Call me when you get into town and get settled at your mother's place. We'll figure out the rest of the details then, and pick out a ring, all that stuff." His dimples popped as he smiled, and Molly felt oddly relaxed and excited at the same time. What on earth had she gotten herself into?

Her last few days of work at the hotel were bittersweet. On Thursday, a group of her colleagues took her out for after-work drinks, and everyone wished her well and told her to hurry back. Ben had already given her the heads-up that Management had approved her leave of absence. He'd assured her that, assuming that everything went the way it was supposed to, she'd still be in line to get promoted to the GM spot when she returned.

Even some of the hotel's regular customers had wished her well. There were a few who had permanent residences on the top floors and Molly had known them now for years. Especially Mrs. Foyle, a very cute and elegant widow in her early eighties. She was still quite active, and had a toy Maltese, Daisy, who traveled all over town with her. Almost every afternoon, around 4pm, Mrs. Foyle came down into the lobby, dressed beautifully and accompanied by Daisy. She made the rounds, saying hello to everyone at the front desk and asking after their families, before heading off to high tea. She met several of her lady friends while out and about, and it was the highlight of her day. On Molly's last day, Mrs. Foyle found her in the lobby and gave her a big hug.

"You'll be missed, my dear. This place has been lucky to have you. I hope you have a lovely adventure, whatever it is that you're off to do." She frowned just a little at that, because all anyone knew was that Molly was heading to Montana because of a personal matter. "And I hope you'll find your way back to us."

"I hope so too! I will miss you and Daisy too. Everyone here has been just wonderful." Molly suddenly felt choked up, her emotions finally catching up with her. The hotel and its people had been in her life for almost ten years. It wasn't easy to just walk away. Molly reminded herself that it was just a temporary situation.

She reminded herself of that again the next day, Friday, as she finished her last shift, and then met her best friend, Meghan, at their favorite small pub in Brooklyn. Harry's Place was just a five-minute walk from her apartment, and Meghan was already seated at a small table in the corner of the bar. The bartender set two glasses of wine down on the table as Molly walked up.

"I hope you don't mind, but I went ahead and ordered a glass of wine for you. The one you usually get, the Shiraz."

"Perfect, thank you." Molly slid into a seat at the table and glanced around the bar. It was packed, as it usually was on a Friday night at 6:30. They were lucky to have gotten a table so quickly.

"I can't believe you're leaving me." Meghan said, with a curious look on her face. "So, fill me in, what's really going on?"

Meghan was actually the only person that Molly had confided in. They'd been best friends since they'd met years ago, when they'd both attended the same high school.

"I've told you everything. I know it's kind of crazy."

"Kind of? You're leaving a career you love to go marry a cowboy in Montana that you've barely talked to since you were fourteen? It's a little strange, you have to admit."

"It's only for six months. I'll be back before you know it."

"Will you though? I wonder."

Meghan had been born and brought up in Brooklyn, and like Molly, worked in Manhattan at a job she loved. She was a lawyer at a small firm that did all kinds of family law and a lot of pro-bono work. She didn't make a lot of money, not the amount you'd usually think of for an attorney, but she loved what she did. Molly knew Meghan was just worried that her best friend was making a huge mistake.

"I know it's an odd situation, but it's strictly a business arrangement. I'll be back in six or seven months, max."

"But how do you benefit from doing this?" Meghan sounded like the lawyer that she was, and Molly smiled. She knew she was just concerned for her.

"I do benefit. I'll be helping an old friend, which will also ensure that the men who work for him and their families will be taken care of. There won't be any layoffs, which there would be if Christian was forced to sell the business. Plus, I'm getting a valuable piece of property, which could be a good, long-term investment." She went on to explain Christian's idea for renovating the property and turning it into an inn.

"That sounds great, but all the more reason why I doubt that you'll be coming back any time soon. You'll be busy running an inn!"

"At first, yes. But by the time six months have passed, I'll have people well trained to run it in my absence. That's what I learned to do here, remember? Manage and train people to do every job necessary to run a busy hotel."

"So, it sounds like you've got it all figured out. I hope this works out for you, I really do." Meghan took a sip of wine, then sighed melodramatically and said, "What if you fall in love with this cowboy, have you considered that?" Molly laughed at this and felt the mood lighten.

"Absolutely not. Christian is just an old friend, and a bit of a playboy." She hesitated for a moment, remembering her intense reaction when their legs had accidentally touched. That couldn't have been real, though. It had to be nerves. Feeling surer of it now, she continued, "This whole thing is just his grandfather's attempt to get him to settle down, but it won't work. We've already talked about it, and Christian made it quite clear that he is not the marrying type. Plus, I can't wait to get back here. Are you kidding? I don't ever want to live anywhere but here."

"Alright then, so now that we've got that all settled, let's plan a wedding. I have to admit, I am curious to visit Beauville and meet everyone."

Except for the fact that she was traveling with four giant suitcases, Molly almost felt like she was going on a long vacation, rather than making an actual move clear across the country. Her apartment was sublet without a hitch, and as she left and gave one final last look, everything was in its place and ready for her to return home. That, at least, was reassuring. In six months, she could come back and pick up as if she'd never been gone.

She was planning to rent a slightly larger car than usual when she arrived in Montana. Her mother and aunt had offered to come get her, but both drove small compact vehicles and there wouldn't be room for her and all her suitcases. They offered to drive separately, but she'd told them that was very sweet, but unnecessary, and she'd just rent something quickly and see them soon.

So, Molly was more than surprised to find someone waiting for her when she got off the plane. Christian was at the gate, and waved at her as she made her way through the crowd.

"Hey there, I talked to your mom, and she said you were planning to rent a car because you have so many bags." His dimples flashed as he teased her.

"Well, I am planning to stay a while. I hope your car is big enough," she teased back.

"Come on, see for yourself." He grabbed hold of the shoulder bag she'd been carrying, and they went down to the baggage carousel to get the rest of her luggage.

Once they got the rest of her bags loaded onto a luggage cart, Christian wheeled them out to the parking lot and down a few rows, until they stopped at a large, slightly dusty truck. Molly watched in admiration as he easily tossed each heavy bag that she'd struggled with earlier into the back of the truck, and then opened the passenger side door for her to climb in.

It was only a little past 6pm, so still plenty light out, and during the forty-five minute drive to Beauville Christian pointed things out here and there. The area hadn't changed much since she'd lived there years ago, but Molly had noticed signs of growth on her last trip and Christian filled her in as they rode along.

"That is a smaller version of the mostly organic market they have in Bozeman, the Community Foods Co-op."

"Over there, that's the only motel in the area, The Sleepy Willow. It's always busy."

Molly glanced at the building as they passed. It was a small motel, nothing fancy, but looked serviceable: an inexpensive, generic place to sleep for a night. She could definitely do better.

"What's that smug smile about?" Molly's expressive face had revealed her thoughts.

"I'm getting ahead of myself, but I was thinking that if that's going to be my only competition, I don't have a lot to worry about. Assuming there's enough business to go around, that is."

"You'll be fine. Rose Cottage will be able to have eight guest rooms, I'm thinking, so while you might not sell out every night, I bet you'll be busy enough."

As they drove through town, Molly noticed how small the town was, and yet bigger than it used to be. Christian explained that Beauville's proximity to Bozeman made the town very appealing to those who wanted to live near the city, but not in it. Beauville had also grown over the years as a popular tourist destination, popular with those who enjoyed fly-fishing and kayaking.

"It looks like business is booming for you too," she commented, as they passed another new development with the Ford Builders sign out front. She knew that, in addition to the ranch and farm work, a good percentage of the Ford family business had evolved into real estate development. Christian had earned a dual degree in architecture and agriculture, which had served him well.

"We can't complain. The demand seems to be steady and growing."

"Your houses are pretty." Molly said, as he slowed down to give her a good look at one of his newest spec houses. Pretty was an understatement. The house was solid and yet light and airy-looking, with lots of windows facing majestic mountains in all directions, as well as gorgeous wood details and natural stone along the walkway.

"Thanks. We try." Christian looked pleased, and Molly realized how little she knew this boy that she'd grown up with. They'd been so close back then, but had grown apart over the years and had never kept in touch after she'd moved to Brooklyn. She had a lot to learn about her old friend.

As they neared the opposite edge of town, Molly noticed that they'd gone past the road that led to her mother's place. She was about to ask where they were going, when they came around the bend and she recognized where they were. She caught her breath, as Christian turned onto the next road and immediately into the driveway of a large sprawling old house that was covered in dusty pink roses.

There was another vehicle parked out front, a navy-blue Acura MX SUV. Christian pulled up next to it and started loading Molly's luggage into the back of the Acura.

"You're going to need a car while you're here," He explained, as he added the last suitcase, shut the door and then handed her the keys. "It's a ranch car, and you'll be staying on the ranch, so it seemed like a no-brainer," he added, as he saw the look on Molly's face, debating whether or not to accept the car. "Think of it like a lease if you like; yours to use as long as you are here. Want to see inside the house?"

"Okay. Yes, of course." Molly said, agreeing to both the car and house at the same time. She followed Christian, as he unlocked the front door and stepped inside.

There was a slight musty smell, and Christian explained that the house hadn't been aired out much in the past year.

"That will disappear quickly, especially once we start on the remodeling and have doors and windows open as we work."

As they walked around Rose Cottage, Molly felt like she was stepping back in time. Most of Christian's grandfather's stuff was still here. When he'd moved in with Christian, he'd left everything exactly as it was, in case he wanted to come back at any time, and she guessed it would have been too hard, too much emotionally, to empty out the house after living here for so many years with his wife.

It had been many years ago, but Molly had been here before, with Christian when they were young. She remembered how much fun his grandfather had been, always so full of life, and how madly in love his grandparents had been. His grandmother had been an amazing cook and there had been always something delicious waiting for them on the counter when they visited, cookies or cupcakes usually. Molly admired the kitchen area, as they entered the room. It needed updating, as the counter tops were all covered with a gold-yellow Formica, that had once been so popular, and the appliances looked original.

"I know for sure that stove needs replacing. Gramps used to complain about it not working half the time, yet he never did anything about it. He didn't do a lot of cooking though."

"There's tons of potential here and it doesn't look like any major work needs to be done."

"No, it's simple stuff." Christian agreed. "Update the kitchen and convert either the family room or living room into a suite. There's another den on the third floor that could be turned into a guestroom, and another room over the garage that was never finished which could be a nice, larger suite."

Molly's mind was swimming with possibilities as they walked back outside.

"Do you want to come for dinner?" She asked impulsively. It was nice of him to make the effort to come get her at the airport, and thoughtful to provide her with the perfect vehicle. Her Aunt Betty always made twice as much food as they needed, so she knew there'd be plenty.

"I'd love to, but I have somewhere I need to be. Prior plans." He didn't explain further than that, which of course made Molly wonder what he was up to. She thanked him again for the ride and the car, and then followed him out of the driveway, watching as he headed in the opposite direction before she headed home.

Chapter 3

"So, what exactly are you telling people?" Aunt Betty asked the next morning over coffee at the Morning Muffin, which, because it was the only breakfast place in town, was totally packed.

"What do you mean?" Molly's aunt often changed topics mid-sentence and it was sometimes hard to keep up, especially today when Molly was still tired from the trip. She was always off-kilter the first day or two home, with the different time zones.

"About this wedding. Are you telling people the truth, or are we supposed to be selling that you're madly in love, even though no one has heard a thing about it until now? Just asking."

Molly took a sip of coffee and considered the question. It was a good one, and she hadn't really thought about it.

"Honestly, I have no idea. I'll have to talk to Christian, I guess. I really hadn't thought beyond actually agreeing to get married and moving here."

"Well, talk to him soon and let us know. People are wondering," Aunt Betty said, as she reached for the carafe of coffee, topped off her cup and then Molly's.

"What people?" Molly asked, as an absolutely gorgeous woman, with long loose dark brown curls and eyes so green they didn't look real, stopped by the table.

"So, this must be Molly," the woman said, looking at Molly's mother and Aunt Betty. "You look just like your mom, and they've said so much about you and your exciting job in the city. I almost feel like I know you."

Molly looked at her mother in surprise. She had no idea who this woman was, yet she seemed to know all about her.

"Honey, this is Isabella Graham. She's a realtor."

"Graham Real Estate is Beauville's top firm. I just had some new cards made up; have one." Isabella fished into her beautiful leather purse, pulled out a gold plated business card case, drew out a card and handed it to Molly, who couldn't help noticing that she also had the most perfectly manicured nails. Molly's were badly neglected and in desperate need of attention.

"We have some beautiful new homes, which just came on the market. Ford Builders did them. Christian does beautiful work."

"I think I know the ones you mean, they are lovely," Molly agreed.

"So what brings you to town?" Isabella asked. Of course, Molly couldn't explain it, and she had a feeling that the less said the better, for some reason. She was by nature a private person, and Isabella's pushiness was rubbing her the wrong way.

"Personal matters; taking some time off to relax and visit for a while."

"Really? Good for you! That must be nice." The waitress arrived just then to deliver her food, and Isabella took the cue to go. "Ladies, I'll leave you to enjoy your breakfast. Molly, hope to see you again while you're in town." She didn't wait for a response and was already half-way across the room, when Molly said softly, "Is it mean of me to say I don't think I like her?"

Aunt Betty laughed at that. "Doesn't surprise me in the least. Isabella is a good kid, but she's a little overbearing at times. Comes with being a competitive sales person, I suppose. She's very good at what she does."

"Wasn't she dating Christian for a while?" her mom asked Aunt Betty, who apparently knew everything about everyone in town.

"Most people would think she still is. I hope Christian has talked with her and given her the heads-up on what's going on." Betty looked thoughtful for a moment. "Makes me wonder though, because if he has, I don't think she would have been that friendly."

Christian had asked for a corner table at Delancey's. He rarely went out for lunch, but given the circumstances and who he was meeting, he thought that Delancey's was the most appropriate spot, and lunch was a safer bet than dinner. Dinner carried different expectations. He really should have had this meeting last week, but it wasn't a conversation he'd been looking forward to having. He checked his watch and—no surprise—she was late. She was always late. Isabella liked to make an entrance.

She swept in ten minutes later, all apologies, and settled down on the plush leather seat next to him. As usual, she looked like a million bucks. She was wearing a cream colored sweater dress that hugged her curves and flattered her olive complexion. Rich red nails and oversized diamond earrings added further polish. Isabella was a beautiful woman and he had enjoyed spending time with her. But, he had been upfront with her from the beginning, that he was not looking for anything serious, and she had said that was fine and that she felt the same. But, if that were true, why was he feeling this ominous sense of dread about having this conversation?

They ordered beverages and then their meals: a steak sandwich with fries for him, and a chopped chicken salad, dressing on the side, for her.

"So, what is so important, that we're having lunch at Delancey's, of all places. I didn't think you did lunch."

"I don't usually. It's just, well, honestly, I meant to have this conversation with you last week, but it's an unusual situation and I don't think you're going to like what I have to say."

"It can't be that bad," she said lightly, and then frowned as realization dawned. "Unless you're breaking up with me."

"Yes. I'm afraid I can't see you anymore." He paused, waiting to see her initial reaction.

Isabella looked stunned, and just stared at him for a long moment before saying, "Why? I thought things were going well?" Isabella had obviously not been expecting this, and to be fair, he hadn't given her any warning.

"It's not you, I know that sounds like the worst cliché, but it's true. Though I was always clear with you that I didn't want anything serious," he reminded her.

"Is there someone else?" Her voice was low and calm, but Christian knew her well enough to know she was absolutely furious. Isabella did not like surprises. She liked being in control, and was usually the one who did the dumping.

"Sort of; it's complicated. I'm actually getting married in about two weeks." When he saw the look of complete shock and horror on Isabella's face, Christian felt like an ass, and decided she deserved to know the whole truth, as bizarre as it was. "It's not someone you know, she's not from around here. Well, she used to be, but that was a long time ago."

"I thought you were never going to get married." Isabella accused him. She didn't appear to be too angry, that was good, but she was definitely confused and who could blame her? He was confused too. He was not happy with his grandfather right now; that was for sure.

The waiter arrived with their meals, and while they ate, Christian filled her in on everything.

"I can't believe your grandfather did that to you, to us. I thought he liked me." Isabella's initial anger was gone, replaced by a sad, vulnerable look as she spoke, and once again Christian cursed his grandfather.

"He did like you. I don't think he really thought this through. It feels like it was an impulsive decision on his part. Though he did know we weren't serious and he definitely didn't approve of that."

"I've met her you know," Isabella said softly, and that surprised Christian. He didn't think she and Molly knew each other. Isabella went on to explain, "Just this morning actually. I stopped for my usual coffee at the Muffin, and she was having breakfast there with her mom and aunt. I know both of the older ladies from the local women's group, and when I said hello, they introduced me. She seems nice."

"She is nice, very nice actually to do this. It's just for six months, then we'll probably go our separate ways."

"Probably? Maybe you'll like being married, fall in love and even want to have kids," Isabella teased.

"That's not even funny. You know me better than that," Christian said.

"I thought that I did. I don't know anything anymore."

Molly made a mental checklist as she drove out to the ranch to meet Christian for dinner and a tour of the grounds. The only thing left on her list was to decide on a dress and the final menu. After they'd finished breakfast at the Morning Muffin, her mother and aunt had dragged her all over town, and then out to Bozeman to meet with caterers and look at dresses for her and her only bridesmaid, Meghan. When they'd finally got home, there'd been a message from Christian inviting her to a casual dinner at the ranch. She'd been tempted to decline, exhausted from the day of running around, but knew it was useless to even suggest, once Aunt Betty had heard the message and then had gone on and on about what a fabulous idea it was for her to see the ranch and get reacquainted with Christian.

When Molly pulled into the driveway, she saw that Christian was sitting on the front porch reading the paper, with an older looking yellow lab curled up at his feet. As Molly walked up to them, the dog wagged its tail and then shuffled over to greet her.

"It's nice to be welcomed so warmly." Molly said, as she reached down to scratch the dog's head. He responded by sitting down and lifting a paw for her.

"He recognizes you. That's pretty amazing after all these years."

"Is this Toby? Why, he must be, what, sixteen by now? I can't believe he's still here with you. How is he?" Molly sat down on the front steps and pulled the dog in for a hug and he muzzled her neck.

"Probably just about sixteen. He just saw the vet last month and got a good report. He's definitely slowing down some, but is still healthy. The vet said he's likely a lab mix, and they tend to live longer than purebreds. Even so, he's an old man, that's for sure."

Toby wagged his tail and looked back at Christian.

"He knows you're talking about him," Molly laughed.

"He's a smart one." Christian stood. "Come on in, I'll show you around."

Molly and Toby followed Christian inside, and followed him around the main house as he pointed out each room. Molly had never been in this building before. It was newer than Rose Cottage.

"When did you build this?" she asked, as Christian led her up to the second floor.

"About twelve years ago. Gramps moved in just a few years later."

The main house wasn't as large as Rose Cottage; there were only four bedrooms here, three upstairs and one down, which was where his grandfather had stayed. The rooms were large and beautifully decorated. Molly brushed her hand against one of the window treatments and sighed at the softness of the material. She was sure Christian hadn't done this himself, but whoever had, had gorgeous taste.

"I hired someone, a local decorator, to come in. I'll be the first to admit I'm clueless about that stuff. I just told her what colors I like and let her do her thing."

"She did amazing work." Each room flowed into the next, the colors soft and inviting without being overly masculine or feminine.

"Thanks, it's Travis' twin sister, Traci. I was going to suggest maybe using her to help with Rose Cottage, if you like?"

"I'd definitely like." Molly beamed at the thought of having the same decorator work her magic with Rose Cottage.

"She'll be at the wedding. I'll introduce you."

Molly's mood shifted as she thought about the wedding. It was nerve-wracking enough to be planning a wedding, but even more so when you barely knew the groom and had never met most of the people who'd be attending.

"Are you sure about the guest list?" Christian had emailed his list of people just that morning, and Molly's aunt had said it seemed to include most of the town. "I don't really have a choice. I've known most of these people all my life; they're either my friends, or people my grandfather knew and would have expected to be there. I have to honor that."

"Even though it's not going to be a real marriage?" That was what troubled Molly.

"It will be a real marriage."

"Yes, technically, but how exactly are we presenting this marriage? Are we supposed to be in love?

"I think so. We have to give that appearance. Even though this is all my grandfather's doing, it's still a real marriage, and that is something that has to be treated with respect."

"Okay, so what's our story then? We have to make sure we're on the same page, as you know people will want to know."

"I know, I've been thinking about that," Christian said, as they walked into the master bedroom, which was large and airy, with a spacious walk-in closet and adjoining master bathroom that held a beautifully tiled glassed- in shower stall and an oversized, old-fashioned, claw-foot soaking tub.

"That's quite a bathroom," Molly breathed. Christian looked pleased.

"Thanks. That was mostly Traci too."

Molly followed Christian downstairs, and into a pretty den-office that was a mix of leather, dark wood and light. The room was at the far end and didn't have a floor above it, but did have a soaring cathedral ceiling with natural wood beams and plenty of glass to let in lots of natural light. Bookcases lined the walls and two oversized club chairs sat on either side of a real wood fireplace. A soft dog bed sat in the middle.

"Toby and I spend a good bit of time here." Upon entering the room, Toby had immediately flopped down in his favorite spot. "Have a seat." Christian sat in one of the club chairs and Molly did the same, enjoying the feel of the buttery soft leather.

"So, what I'm thinking is that we keep it simple. Remind people that we knew each other way back when we were kids, and say I ran into you in New York when I was there on a business trip a few months ago. What's the name of your hotel, the Carlyle?"

"Clarendon."

"Right. I can say I stayed there, ran into you. Saw you again when you came home to visit your mom, and that we've been in touch since." He frowned. "At least there's an element of truth there."

"It doesn't sound very romantic though, not if you want people to believe we're madly in love."

"Okay, you're right." He thought for a moment, then said, "I know, how about this: I ran into your mom and aunt, told them I was heading to New York on business and they insisted that I look you up."

Molly smiled. "Now that is believable. Aunt Betty would have demanded it."

Christian grinned, and Molly thought how young he looked when he let loose a little, and how attractive he was when he smiled, and the laugh lines danced around the corners of his mouth and eyes.

"So, I looked you up and we went to your favorite restaurant for dinner, where was that?"

"Becco, near Times Square. We had steak and the triple side of pasta."

"That sounds good. We're having steak tonight too, no pasta though, just baked potato, I'm afraid." His eyes twinkled, and Molly realized she was having fun. She was starting to remember what a good time she and Christian always had together.

"I love baked potatoes."

"Great, so where was I? Okay, so we went to your favorite restaurant, and as soon as I met you there I was a nervous wreck. I was remembering a tomboy with short brown hair and freckles, and in walks this drop-dead gorgeous girl with long caramel curls and a beautiful smile. The only way I knew it was you was because of the freckles. They're very cute by the way. How's that?"

Drop-dead gorgeous? Christian was being too generous. "Good, but remember, you want this to be believable."

"Molly, you are gorgeous. You must know that." Christian looked so serious that Molly was surprised.

She had never thought of herself as gorgeous, just as someone who cleaned up okay when lots of makeup and clothes were involved.

"Okay, continue…" she encouraged.

"So, I was surprised by how well Molly had grown up, but it was when we got to chatting over dinner that I realized I was falling head over heels for her. I felt like I'd known her forever, and yet was just starting to learn who she was. That's how it started, and she felt the same. She came to Beauville a few times, and I went to NY a few more times, and we both realized that it was just too hard being so far apart, and that there was no reason to wait. We went back to her favorite restaurant on my last trip to the city, and over champagne and chocolate mousse, I popped the question and much to my delight, she said yes!" He was really getting into it, and Molly thought that if the farming thing ever didn't work out, he could make a living acting.

"That was quite a performance! You convinced me. They'll eat it up."

"Let's hope so. You hungry yet? I can throw the steaks on the grill."

Molly's stomach rumbled in response, eliciting a chuckle from Christian.

"Come on out to the kitchen. The baked potatoes are already on the grill and the steaks are ready to go."

"Can I do anything to help?" Molly offered, as they made their way to the kitchen. She'd already admired this room earlier, when Christian started the tour. It was a true chef's kitchen, complete with granite counter tops, double ovens and an Aga stove.

"Actually, I have a bag of lettuce and some veggies out on the counter for salad. If you want to chop the veggies and throw everything in a bowl, that'd be great. Oh, and there's a bottle of Cabernet next to the fridge that I opened earlier; feel free to pour us both a glass if you like."

Christian grabbed the steaks and headed off to the grill, while Molly got to work opening the bottle of Cabernet and pouring two glasses. She then sliced a juicy beefsteak tomato and chopped a red pepper, then prepared some onion and cucumber. She emptied the bag of lettuce into a bowl, added the vegetables and then tossed until they were well mixed.

She took a sip of the wine and it was delicious. A few minutes later Christian returned with the steaks, and they sat down to dinner. While they ate, Christian filled her in on the Ford business ventures.

"It's a working ranch, about five thousand acres in total. About half the men we employ work as ranchers, the other half are with the building side of the business. We are general contractors and I'm a licensed architect. I've grown that side of the business since graduating college. The ranch side has stayed fairly steady. That's not where our long-term growth is likely to be."

"Do you do mostly large developments or single projects?"

"It's a mix right now. It used to be all single projects, but over the years the development side has grown so that it's now almost half of what we do. Beauville still has a lot of land and plenty of demand."

"So, business is good?" Molly was happy for him. Christian had always said he was going to be an architect, and he'd done it.

"We can't complain. We're one of the larger employers in town. Beauville is still very much a small town. It's a great place to live."

After dinner, Christian took the bottle of wine outside and they sat on the front porch sofa, chatting comfortably, with Toby contentedly sprawled on the front step.

"We'll be expected to immediately leave the next day for our honeymoon," Christian said.

Molly hadn't thought that far ahead, and wondered what he had in mind. She had a feeling he wouldn't want to do anything typical, such as Hawaii or the Caribbean. That would be a little too romantic.

"I was thinking, if it sounds good to you, we could spend a week in New York City? You can show me around. Might be kind of fun, I've never really seen much of the city."

"That would be great!" Molly was thrilled with the idea. There was so much to see and do in New York, and it was always fun to play tourist and see the city through someone else's eyes.

They chatted a bit longer, and watched the sun set. It was a beautiful night, clear and crisp, and Molly reluctantly decided it was time for her to head home. She was surprised at what a good evening she'd had, and how much she'd enjoyed Christian's company. Maybe the next six months would be better than she'd thought. It looked like she and Christian might be able to pick up their strong friendship from where they'd left off.

"I should probably get going. I have to get up early tomorrow, and I'm sure you do too." Molly stood and picked up her glass.

"Here, I'll take that." Christian took her glass and the wine bottle and carried them inside, returning just a moment later to walk her to her car.

"I'm glad you could come out tonight. It was really good to catch up. Reminded me a little of the old days."

"I know, for me too. Thanks for dinner, I really had a good time."

Christian pulled her in for a quick hug and, once again, Molly felt that surge of electricity when they touched. The intensity of it startled her and she pulled back awkwardly, wondering if it was all in her mind, or if Christian had felt it too. His face gave nothing away, and Molly told herself it must have been the second glass of wine playing tricks on her.

Chapter 4

Molly and her mother set out the next morning for Bozeman again, in search of a wedding dress. They'd run out of time the day before and hadn't got to the last store on their list. Aunt Betty wasn't able to join them this time; she had a long-standing hair appointment that she didn't want to miss. As much as she loved her aunt, it was nice for Molly to have her mom all to herself. Her mother was much quieter than Aunt Betty, content to stay in the background and a bit more relaxing to be around.

"Do you ever miss the city?" Molly asked as her mother pulled into the parking lot of the dress shop.

"Of course I do. I loved living there. It's a different world, so alive, there's always something to do and things going on. But I love it here too. I always have. It was just too much after your father passed on. I needed that time away and moving to Brooklyn was the perfect solution. I think I always knew I'd want to come back here someday."

"Now Aunt Betty loves it too. I never thought she'd leave Brooklyn."

"I don't think she would have, if it hadn't been for Harold getting sick."

Aunt Betty's husband of nearly thirty years had been sick with colon cancer for several years before passing away. By the time he'd died, Betty had already started the grieving process and had had some time to process it.

"It was all her idea, coming back here," her mother said softly. "I talked about Beauville a lot and she knew I missed it, and I think she was at the point where she wanted a fresh start, too. There were too many memories of Harold in Brooklyn. It definitely helped me to get out of Beauville when I left, and I think we both knew it would help us to come back here."

"It seems like she's settled in well."

"That's an understatement! It's as if she's lived here her whole life. She's already met more people in the two years we've been here, than I ever did in all my years with your father." They both smiled at that as they got out of the car and walked in the store.

Molly hoped that her mother and aunt would eventually find someone else. They were only in their early sixties and were adorable. Her mother was about the same size as Molly, a few inches over five feet, and was still a size six, same as Molly. She wore her hair in a pretty bob that just grazed her collar bone, and she and Aunt Betty colored their hair regularly to hide any trace of gray. Her mom's color was a soft sandy shade, a little lighter than Molly's, while her Aunt Betty wore hers a touch longer and in layered curls that were a brighter blonde. Aunt Betty was taller and a bit rounder than both of them, but hid the extra weight well as she was more into fashion than Molly's mom, or even Molly for that matter.

A cheerful saleswoman noticed them immediately and came over to help.

"We called yesterday. I'm the one who needs a dress as soon as possible. My wedding is less than two weeks away."

"Wonderful! I'm Emily; we spoke on the phone. I set a few dresses aside for you, ones that we have in stock. So if you like any of them, we can alter it within the week for you."

"That sounds perfect!" Molly wasn't about to be too picky, given the circumstances, and had already decided that she was going to choose something today, from this store, and be done with it.

So, she wasn't expecting to love all three dresses that Emily brought out to show her. They were all beautiful and simple, exactly what she had in mind.

She modeled each one, and though she and her mom liked them all, they both agreed on the winner. When Molly walked out of the dressing room in the third dress, her mother caught her breath and her eyes teared up.

"You like this one, I take it?" Molly said, as she walked toward the mirror and felt goose-bumps as she saw her image. The dress looked as though it had been made for her. It fit perfectly, and was both elegant and simple. It was a timeless design and Molly loved it.

The enormity of what she was about to do really hit her for the first time, as she stood staring at herself in the wedding dress. A wedding dress! Something in her expression must have alerted her mother because she walked over to Molly and took her hand.

"You look breathtakingly beautiful in that dress. But, you don't have to do this." She spoke softly but firmly, and Molly looked at her in confusion.

"You know why I'm doing this, Mom. It's just for six months, and Christian is a nice guy. It'll be fine." She reassured her.

"I just don't want you to feel pressured into something you don't want to do. Rick will be fine if something happens to his job. He'll land on his feet."

"He might, but what about the others? What about Christian? He's worked too hard to get to this point. He doesn't deserve to have everything taken away."

"I'm just saying, if you don't want to do this, you don't have to. Your aunt and I will support you, no matter what. You know that."

"I know, Mom. I do want to do this though. It feels like the right thing, if that makes sense?"

Her mother just squeezed her hand and then pulled her for a tight hug.

"I'm so proud of you, honey."

There was no bachelor party. Unless you counted the night before the wedding, when Travis and Christian spent most of the evening in Christian's den, sitting by the fire, with Toby in his usual spot. They drank scotch, a fair amount of a very good blend that Travis had brought over.

"I've been saving this for a special occasion. Guess this is as good as any."

The scotch was smooth and strong and began to take the edge off Christian's nerves, which had been jumpy all day. All week in fact.

"So, you're really going through with it?" Travis gave his friend a searching look. "You sure about this?"

Christian was silent for a long moment. "Sure about it? No. It's a god- awful situation my grandfather put me in. A heck of a thing to do to Molly, too. She doesn't deserve this. It's six months of her life she's giving up, getting stuck with me."

"Six months isn't really that long in the whole scheme of things. Gives her a chance to spend some time with her family. Her aunt told me they've hardly seen her in the past few years since they moved out here. Molly never got much time off, only made it out here once a year around Christmas, and even then it wasn't on the holiday itself. Hotels are open on holidays and, as a manager, she was usually there."

Christian had never thought about that. "No kidding. That must have been hard on her and her family." Holidays had always been a big deal in his house growing up. His mother had been an excellent cook and his dad had made a great Santa. He'd had the rounded belly to pull it off. Christian's eyes darkened as he thought of them. They had lost their lives much too young and so quickly. Even worse, it had happened on Christmas Eve, as they had been on their way home. A drunk driver going the wrong way on a dark mountain road. They'd never seen it coming, and had died instantly. It had happened nearly fifteen years ago, but sometimes the hurt was still so raw and fresh that he couldn't believe it had been that long.

He didn't know what he would have done without his grandparents. His grandfather had been a rock and his grandmother had kept all the holiday traditions going. When she'd passed and his grandfather had moved in with him, he'd done the same. Yeah, holidays were important, and he couldn't imagine missing them. His younger brother Dan, though, couldn't stand Christmas to this day, because of what had happened.

"Earth to Christian," Travis teased.

"Sorry, just spaced out there for a minute." He knew that Travis understood. They'd been best friends since elementary school.

"So, what did you decide to do for a honeymoon? Anything?"

"Manhattan. I thought it would be fun for Molly, well, for both of us actually, to play tourist there. She knows the city so well and I've barely seen anything."

"That's a good idea. Two friends who happen to be married visiting the big city." Travis smiled mischievously before adding, "What about sleeping arrangements?"

"What about them?"

"Molly's a beautiful girl. I'm just saying."

Christian frowned. "It's not like that."

"So are you saying you're going to be celibate for the next six months?"

"I'm not saying anything. To be honest, I haven't thought that far ahead."

"Fair enough. What about Isabella? You said she's the only other person who knows the truth about your wedding?"

"I thought I owed her that much. She's a good person; we had fun together."

"Well, if she knows the truth, maybe she'd be up for an occasional rendezvous?"

Christian shut that idea right down. "Absolutely not. I wouldn't do that to either of them. Wouldn't be right."

"I suppose not." Travis had a thoughtful look on his face.

"So that means Isabella is available? Would it be breaking guy-code if I took her out? Not saying I'm going to, just wondering."

Christian grinned at that, and realized he didn't have the slightest jealous feeling about it. He really did like Isabella and he loved Travis. The thought of the two of them together was intriguing. "Go for it. I am totally okay with that idea."

There wasn't an official bachelorette party either. Meghan arrived around six the night before the wedding, and she and Molly were quickly shooed out of the house by Aunt Betty, who said they had the rest of their lives to stay home.

They decided to go to Delancey's and have dinner at the bar. Delancey's was not only the best restaurant in town, it also had entertainment, and tonight it was two guys on guitars singing Top 40 covers. They were pretty good, though, and the music made for nice background sounds as they ate dinner and caught up.

"I can't believe you're really doing this." Meghan said, as the bartender set down her cocktail, a shimmery pink Cosmopolitan.

"Neither can I." Molly raised her glass of Chardonnay and tapped it against Meghan's drink. "Cheers."

"Cheers. I do think you're a little crazy for doing this, but in a good way. And you're right, six months will go fast. I'll have you back in Brooklyn before I know it. Right?"

Molly felt herself relax a little. Everything was taken care of for the wedding, and her best friend was here. Now she could just try to enjoy the party that it was sure to be.

"Yes, absolutely. How is everything back home? Any good gossip?"

Meghan thought for a minute. "Actually, I ran into your boss from the hotel, Ben, as I was leaving Harry's place on Tuesday. He said to say hello, and that the renovations are coming along beautifully. Said you won't recognize the place by the time you get back. Sounds exciting."

"It should be amazing when it's finished. I can't wait to see it."

"So, let's talk about what's going on now. Tell me more about this man you're about to marry. Will I like him?"

Molly laughed a little. "Yes, you'll like him, he's a really great guy. The more time I spend with him, the more I'm seeing the childhood friend I used to know. He still has the same dog, Toby." She went on to explain the history of Toby.

"That's so sweet, that you used to share a dog. Amazing that he's still around. It's been, what, fifteen years at least?"

"Sixteen, actually."

"So, he's a nice guy. Is he good looking, at all?"

"He is. I almost didn't recognize him at first. He's gotten so tall, must be about six-foot-two, and he's in great shape from working outside so much." Molly thought about Christian's face; it was hard to describe. "He's not classically gorgeous, you're not going to stop and stare, but he's attractive enough. Great hair and nice eyes. You know, he's someone you can trust."

"Hmmm, guess I'll have to decide for myself." Meghan was quiet for a moment, before adding, "What if it works out? Imagine if you fall in love with your husband! How cool would that be?"

"Complicated is more like it. I can't see that happening though. I don't think there's any vibe there for either of us. I do enjoy his company, but it's more like we've picked up our friendship where it was left off, and that's ideal, really. It will make for a smooth six months, and then I can return to life as I used to know it."

"I'll toast to that!" They clinked glasses once again and then turned their attention to dinner, as the bartender set two hot plates of sizzling steaks in front of them.

The wedding went off without a hitch. Molly was surprised that she was as nervous as she imagined a real bride would be, as Meghan helped her get into her bridal dress and fixed her hair in an elegant French twist, leaving a few pieces loose to frame the side of her face. She could understand how brides often dropped ten pounds or so right before the wedding. There were so many little details that had to be taken care of, even with a smaller, last minute affair like this. Of course her hotel training had helped immeasurably, and her mother and aunt were on top of everything, as well. Molly was anxious to get the ceremony over with, so she could relax and unwind at the wedding reception.

They held the wedding service at a nearby chapel, with a justice of the peace. It hadn't felt right to Molly to do it in a formal church setting, given the circumstances, and Christian had understood. The chapel was beautiful, and had plenty of room for all of their guests. Molly estimated that their 'intimate small wedding' was going to come in at just over two hundred attendees, most of whom she barely knew. Christian's brother, Dan, wasn't there, though. He was out of the country on an assignment for one of the financial magazines that he occasionally wrote for. He'd offered to try and postpone his trip or even cancel, but Christian had told him not to bother, since it wasn't a 'real' wedding. At the moment though, it felt very real, and quite strange, to Molly.

Since her father wasn't here to walk her down the aisle, Molly had asked both her mother and aunt to do the honors. They'd loved the idea, and now stood on either side of her, arms linked with hers as she followed her sole bridesmaid, Meghan, down the aisle. Meghan looked beautiful, with her long blonde hair pulled back into a tumble of curls that cascaded to her shoulders. She wore an elegant and simple sheath in a flattering pale blue shade, which seemed like a good choice for a spring wedding.

Her mother and Aunt Betty had chosen their own dresses. Her mother's was a soft blue-gray shimmery fabric, and her aunt's a brighter silvery shade. They both looked terrific, and had glistening eyes as they walked beside Molly.

Christian and Travis, his best man, were waiting for them, and they both looked so distinguished and serious. But as they got closer, Christian smiled and his eyes lit up. The whole moment felt surreal to Molly, as she said her vows and agreed to love, honor, and cherish the man standing in front of her: her friend.

The chaplain pronounced them man and wife, and told Christian to kiss his bride. He did, and though it was a quick peck in front of a crowd of people, Molly was surprised by how much she liked the feel of his lips on hers. It shook her for a moment; she hadn't been expecting to feel anything remotely like attraction. She dismissed the feeling immediately though, chalking it up to the excitement of the moment.

Christian took her hand and led the way through the crowd and to the waiting limousine outside. Travis, Meghan, and her mother and Aunt Betty joined them, and they rode a few miles down the road to the reception. It was to be held at the Beauville country club and the buffet catered by a local company that Christian had recommended.

The food was wonderful. They had decided to go with several stations, so people could have a selection of options. There was a carving station with several meats, a pasta station and a hot station with stuffed shrimp, sautéed chicken and wild salmon. Everyone raved about the food, and seemed to have a good time.

Molly barely ate a thing. She was too busy going from table to table, greeting her guests and, in many cases, meeting them for the first time too. Her Uncle Richard was there, of course, and she'd made her mother promise not to tell him the truth, especially as he still worked for Christian. She felt a little guilty about that, as she did about the fact that everyone was so nice and seemed so happy for Christian and for her. She sensed that they approved of his choice, which both flattered her and made her feel a little sad at the same time.

Aunt Betty was the belle of the ball. She was having a blast and reveling in all the attention. Her mother seemed to be enjoying herself as well, as she relaxed at her table and took it all in, as was her way.

Once everyone was fed and the cake was cut, the entertainment started. The band they'd found on such short notice was excellent and soon had the crowd up and on the dance floor. Meghan stayed out there almost the entire time and made sure Molly was dancing up a storm as well. Molly loved to dance, too, and even succeeded in dragging her mother up for a few songs. Aunt Betty was the first one on the dance floor and the last to leave. It seemed as though a good time was certainly had by all.

Christian wasn't much of a dancer. He joined Molly for the official first dance, and then danced once with her mother and then her aunt. After that, he mostly sat out and visited with various friends and family members. Molly noticed that Travis danced quite a bit, though, especially with Meghan, who seemed to be really enjoying herself, which Molly was glad to see.

By the time the music stopped, Molly was exhausted. She and Christian said their goodbyes to everyone as they all walked out. The limo was still out front waiting for them, but this time just Molly and Christian got in and, less than ten minutes later, they arrived at Christian's house and Molly's new home for the next six months.

Christian had come by the day before to pick up Molly's things, so her suitcases were waiting for her in the guest room. Molly had admired this room when she'd first seen it the day she'd visited, and Christian had shown her around. The guest room was almost as large as the master bedroom. It was decorated in soft peach and cream tones, and while it didn't have a walk-in closet, it did have plenty of hanging space and, like the master bedroom, a beautiful, large bathroom with heated marble tile floors, a glassed-in shower and an oversized soaking tub. The bathroom closet was also stocked with plenty of thick towels, shampoo and conditioner. It was almost like being in a hotel, Molly thought to herself. She had everything she needed.

Christian walked her upstairs and stopped outside her door.

"Well, goodnight Mrs. Ford. Get a good night's sleep, we have to be up early tomorrow for our flight to New York."

"Mrs. Ford. That's going to take a little getting used to."

"You have to admit, it has a nice ring to it."

"Goodnight Christian." He gave her a warm hug and a kiss on the forehead. Oddly, Molly felt a little disappointed, surprised to admit she'd been wishing he'd aimed for her lips instead.

Chapter 5

Molly and Christian got up early the next morning, and flew into LaGuardia that afternoon to begin their honeymoon. Christian had booked them into an upscale bed and breakfast in Manhattan. He'd explained that he thought it would give Molly some ideas to keep in mind as they renovated Rose Cottage. The property was lovely, and their suite had two bedrooms with a cozy living room in the middle and a pretty gas fireplace. Each bedroom had its own bathroom, and they were elegant, mostly contemporary, though with old-fashioned touches such as claw-foot tubs. Several candles rested on a shelf by the tub, and Molly was looking forward to a soaking session and a chance to catch up on her stack of to-be-read novels.

Their suite also had high speed internet hook up, and shortly after they arrived Christian plugged in his laptop to check email and return any emergency calls, of which there were several.

"Didn't you tell them you were on vacation?" Molly asked, as his phone had rung non-stop since they got off the plane.

"Yes, this is slow, believe it or not." He grinned as his phone rang again. "Sorry, I'll forward all calls to Tricia in the office, and she can just put through the ones that are true emergencies."

Molly left him alone for a bit to deal with his flurry of calls, and retreated to her bedroom to start unpacking and getting organized for the week. They had a busy schedule and there was a lot to fit in. Christian's office manager, Tricia, had done a great job of getting them tickets to shows and events that were known to be sold out months in advance, such as The Book of Mormon, which Molly had been dying to see. Many of the guests at the Clarendon had raved about it, but Molly had never been able to get seats. With her schedule, she could never plan far in advance for things like that, and though she'd tried several times on her nights off, there were never last-minute tickets available.

An hour later, Christian tapped on her door, and they ventured out for this first night together in Manhattan. Tricia had worked a true miracle for this evening, somehow managing to score them a table at Per Se, the famous Thomas Keller restaurant that was usually booked out at least a month in advance. Molly had never been here before, though she had dreamed of it. Per Se was a special occasion restaurant, and even if she could have managed to get a reservation, it was way out of her budget. Per Se was famous for its exquisite food and its nine-course tasting menu, and had made every top restaurant list in the world.

They started with the restaurant's famous *oysters and pearls*, an unusual pairing of tapioca and fresh Duxbury oysters. It sounded like an odd combination, but was one of the only dishes that never came off the menu, due to customer demand. After one bite, Molly could see why. The unique flavors swirled and combined to bring out the best of each ingredient.

They sipped champagne to start, and moved on to a half bottle of white wine to complement the poached lobster and then, later on, a half bottle of Pinot Noir selected by the sommelier to perfectly match the pressed duck.

One course flowed into the next and, over the next few hours, Molly and Christian fully caught up on each other's lives.

"When I graduated college, I worked for a construction company in Billings for a few years, learned the ropes and then moved home to Beauville at my grandfather's urging. He always wanted me to take over the ranch and we agreed to expand into construction and development, once I had the experience."

"How was it, working with your grandfather?"

"It was great." Christian smiled, thinking of his grandfather. Molly knew he must be missing him often. It had only been a few weeks since he passed. "I learned a ton from him."

"So, have you always been a confirmed bachelor?" Molly teased him, as she took another bite of the refreshing raspberry sorbet that had just been served.

"Actually, no. I was engaged years ago, when I was living in Billings. It didn't work out."

Molly was surprised to hear this, but didn't say anything in response, figuring he'd say more if he wanted to. She continued eating her sorbet in silence, and after a few minutes, Christian continued.

"We went to college together. I was head over heels for Heather and thought she felt the same. I guess I was just too young to see the signs." He glanced up from his chocolate cheesecake and met Molly's eyes. She saw something dark and raw reflected there.

"She broke up with me two weeks before the wedding. I was crushed. Never saw it coming. She said she just didn't love me enough." He smiled bitterly and a muscle in his jaw flickered. It was clear to Molly that Christian didn't like to dredge up this particular memory.

"So that's why you don't want to get too serious with anyone." Molly could understand.

"No, that's not it. Well, maybe partly. I guess it just made me think. Maybe Heather was on to something. How do you know when you love someone 'enough'? Easier to just not go there. To just take things one day at a time and enjoy life. Never let it get too messy, you know?"

"I get it." Molly raised her glass, and Christian did the same. "To clean living, no mess!" she said, as they clinked glasses. Molly was smiling, but inside she felt a little sad for Christian. He was still young to be so cynical about love.

"So what's your story? Are you as screwed up romantically as I am?" His tone was light and teasing, but Molly could sense an underlying seriousness too. It was a fair question.

"I suppose I probably am," she admitted. "I really haven't seriously dated anyone in years. I've just been so focused on work, and my schedule doesn't make it easy either. I'm always filling in at the last minute, working holidays and nights. Not quite as glamorous as it seems."

"But you love it." It was a statement, not a question, and Molly was glad to see that Christian understood how she felt about her work.

"Yeah, I do love it. I started there when I was sixteen, at the front desk, and worked part-time all through high school and college, and fell in love with the business. I'm lucky in that I really love what I do for work; it's not just a job."

Christian kept his phone under control for the rest of the week, and Molly was surprised at what a great time they had, and how fast the week went by. She'd been a little nervous that so much time together might produce more than one of those awkward stretches of silence, when you run out of things to say and each person is desperately trying to think of something to keep the conversation alive. It wasn't like that for them, though, and for that Molly was grateful. They had plenty of quiet stretches, but it felt like the comfortable silence between friends and family, when you could enjoy each other's company without saying anything at all.

Molly had loved showing Christian all around her beloved Manhattan. Each time she showed someone all of her favorite places, it was like seeing them again for the first time. They even took in a Knicks' game, which was a first for Molly, as well. She'd been to several Yankees and Mets' games over the years, but hadn't followed basketball much, so hadn't bothered with the Knicks. Christian loved it though, and he was pleased to be able to introduce her to something new. She was surprised by how much she enjoyed it. They had good seats and it was a close game, with a last second win by the Knicks.

Before she knew it, they were back in Beauville. The week in New York had been fun and familiar, as they'd been in what felt like her home town. Now that they were in Beauville, Molly was feeling less comfortable and a bit nervous about how the next six months would unfold. It was somewhat unsettling to be living in someone else's home. They'd never actually discussed the details of what their day-to-day living arrangements would be like. Her room was lovely, but she didn't really feel at home here, not yet.

Her first day at the ranch ended up being a bit of a disaster too. Molly spent a good twenty minutes searching every cabinet in the kitchen for coffee, before finally finding it around the corner in a small pantry. She'd just settled on a stool at the kitchen island with the newspaper and a mug of coffee when Christian came through the door. It was a few minutes past seven and he looked like he'd been out working for several hours already.

"What time did you get up today?" She asked.

"About five, same as always. I make the rounds on the ranch, jump in the shower, grab a bite to eat, and then head to the office for the rest of the day." He proceeded to do exactly that, while Molly helped herself to a second cup of coffee and thought about the lazy day ahead that she had planned. She was still tired from their trip; flying always did that to her, and was actually looking forward to just settling in and maybe visiting with her mom and aunt later in the afternoon.

She was just about done with her coffee and about to head upstairs to shower and change, when a fifty-something year old woman strolled into the kitchen and then stopped short when she saw Molly.

"You must be Molly," the woman stated. She didn't look too pleased about it.

"Mrs. O'Brien?" Christian had given Molly the heads-up that he had a housekeeper, who came by several times a week. Mrs. O'Brien was in her late fifties, a grandmother of three, and had worked for Christian and his grandfather before him for over twenty years. She had two married daughters, and thought of

Christian and his younger brother Dan as the sons she never had. He'd actually invited her to the wedding, but she'd been unable to attend as she was on vacation that week, on a cruise that her children had booked for her many months ago, as a Christmas gift. Molly hadn't yet had a chance to meet her until today. "That would be me." She said, and set her purse down in the corner of the room before turning her attention back to Molly. "Did you need something?"

Molly took that as her cue to leave. "No, I was just going."

"Okay then." She watched as Molly rinsed out her cup, placed it in the dishwasher and then walked quickly down the hall. Molly wondered exactly what Christian had told her about their marriage, because this woman wasn't exactly welcoming.

Molly got ready, and then went off to spend the day visiting with her mother and aunt. They were having their morning coffee when she arrived. She accepted another cup, joined them at the kitchen table and told them about her first meeting with Mrs. O'Brien.

"So, I don't think she likes me."

"Linda's a nice person," her mother said. "A little stiff until you get to know her, but don't forget, she's been taking care of that family for over twenty years. She's not used to having another woman around."

"I didn't think of that." Molly hoped Mrs. O'Brien would warm up to her; it would be a bit rocky if she didn't.

She spent the rest of the day with her mom and Aunt Betty in Bozeman. They drove out there and had a great lunch at a local café, and spent the afternoon roaming around the shops, mostly window-shopping, but Molly did pick up a few cute tops and a new pair of cowboy boots. She'd noticed that people dressed more casually out here compared to New York, and just about everyone liked to wear boots. Molly found a buttery-soft caramel-colored pair that were the most comfortable she'd ever owned.

She returned to the ranch at a few minutes past four, and called out hello to Mrs. O'Brien who was vacuuming the front hallway when she walked in. Mrs. O'Brien turned the vacuum off for a moment, muttered hello back and then raised an eyebrow at the armful of bags Molly was carrying.

"Bargain shopping in Bozeman." Molly said apologetically, and then slunk upstairs to put her things away. Why did she feel guilty about enjoying an afternoon and doing a little shopping? Probably because it was something she so rarely did. She glanced at the clock in her room: Christian had said he'd be home around five. She had just under an hour and she needed to keep busy. She decided to venture down to the kitchen to make something delicious. Puttering around the kitchen always relaxed her.

Mrs. O'Brien was nowhere to be found when Molly entered the kitchen, and then she heard footsteps directly above her.

Good, she was on a different floor entirely, so she'd have the kitchen to herself for a bit. So, what to make? She opened the refrigerator and just stared inside it for a solid minute, contemplating her options. There was a package of ground beef, some eggs, parmesan cheese. She checked the cabinets in the pantry and found a large can of crushed tomatoes, onions, garlic, plenty of pasta and a loaf of bread. Perfect, she'd make her famous meatballs and sauce. It was one of her favorite meals and something that always came out great.

She got the sauce started first, finding a large saucepan and a sharp knife and cutting board, and quickly peeled and chopped a large onion and a few cloves of garlic, then added them into the saucepan with a bit of olive oil, just enough to coat the bottom of the pan. She turned the heat on medium and then found a large mixing bowl to make the meatballs in.

For the meatballs, she just dumped in the ground beef, cracked in an egg, tore up a few slices of bread and added a few shakes of Italian seasoning, and salt and pepper. She formed the meat into balls and baked them on a cookie sheet in the oven for twenty minutes, and then plopped them all into the saucepan to simmer for another twenty. She cooked up a box of spaghetti and was just pouring the pasta into a colander to drain, when Mrs. O'Brien and Christian walked into the kitchen together at the same time.

"What are you doing?" Mrs. O'Brien's voice was oddly calm, and Molly suddenly felt nervous.

"Just making dinner."

"That's my job." She flung open the refrigerator and then turned back to Molly. "You used the ground beef," she accused.

"I made meatballs."

"I was going to make American Chop Suey. I was just about to start it so it would be ready for when Christian wants dinner." She glared at Molly and then glanced at Christian.

"That's my fault. I don't think I told Molly that you usually do the cooking for me."

"I *always* do the cooking," Mrs. O'Brien corrected.

"I'm sorry," Molly apologized, then added, "so maybe today you get to go home early?"

Mrs. O'Brien just grunted at that, then stomped off and, moments later, they heard the front door slam behind her.

"I really don't think she likes me." Molly said again.

"She just doesn't know you. She'll come around." Christian looked exhausted. Molly knew she would be too, if she'd started as early as he did.

"Are you hungry?"

"Not yet. I'm sure I will be by the time I change out of these clothes and finish up some paperwork in my den. Say, fifteen minutes or so? It smells great."

Christian was back as predicted in about fifteen minutes, and looked much more comfortable in a pair of old sweats and a long-sleeved tee-shirt. Molly found a couple of shallow bowls and put some pasta and a few meatballs in each, and then they sat at the island bar.

Christian inhaled his food and went back for more, before Molly was even half-done with hers. He hadn't mentioned if he liked the meatballs, but since he'd gone back for more they must have been okay. People usually raved about them. After they finished, Molly went to clear the dishes but Christian stopped her.

"I'll do it. You don't have to wait on me," he snapped, and Molly sat back in surprise. She hadn't yet seen this grouchy, moody side of him. Molly had already put the rest of the meatballs and pasta in the refrigerator and cleaned the serving dishes, so all Christian had to do was to rinse their plates and put them in the dishwasher. She wondered if the stress of their arrangement was catching up to him.

"Do you want to watch some TV?" he asked in a more friendly tone, and she nodded. She was starting to feel a bit awkward again—that sense of being displaced when you're a guest in someone else's house and you'd so much rather be home in your own bed, your own apartment. She sighed. There was still a good six months to go, she'd better settle in and make the best of it.

She followed Christian into the family room and settled into one corner of the oversized leather sofa. Christian sat on the opposite far side and clicked on the TV. It automatically landed on a sports channel and a basketball game, and Christian watched for a minute before turning to Molly. "You probably don't really want to watch this though, do you?"

Molly hesitated for a second; watching basketball on TV would probably be at the bottom of her list, but she wanted to be polite. "This is fine."

Christian waited a second and then flicked the channel to see what else was on, before finally settling on Showtime and a new episode of Homeland. Molly smiled to herself. Christian must have remembered that she'd told him it was one of her favorite shows.

A half-hour later, totally lost in the show, she happened to glance Christian's way and saw that he was sound asleep.

After about a week, they settled into a routine of sorts. Molly had always been an early riser, but Christian gave that word new meaning. He was up before five most mornings and out the door a half hour later, off to meet his men on the ranch. He'd pop back by around seven or so, would grab a bite to eat, then head out again, stopping first at the Ford Builders office on Main Street, just a block down the road from Travis' law firm. Tricia, his office manager, would arrive by eight and they'd meet briefly to go over his schedule and any pending business from the day before. By eight-thirty, Christian was back on the road again and heading to one of their many development sites.

Molly usually rose around six-thirty and joined Christian for coffee and breakfast around seven. After that, she often sat in the study for a bit, curled up in one of the soft club chairs and read the paper, while Toby slept at her feet. It was her favorite time of day, when the house was quiet and she had the whole day ahead of her to dream and plan for what Rose Cottage could become. She also tried to stay out of the way of Mrs. O'Brien, though after that first awkward day, they had settled into a truce of sorts. Molly let her do all the cooking and raved about it each time. Molly could sense that Mrs. O'Brien was starting to thaw a bit; she'd even cracked a smile the day before. That was something.

Sometimes Christian came home for lunch, but more often than not, she was on her own and just grabbed a quick sandwich or light salad, before heading to Rose Cottage for the afternoon

In the past week, Christian's team of men had already started on the remodeling. They were tackling the upstairs rooms first, then would be converting the room over the garage and the family room on the first floor, turning each area into a small suite, everyone with its own bathroom.

Molly was excited for today, because she was meeting with Travis's twin sister, Traci, to go over ideas for redecorating. Traci had stopped by Rose Cottage earlier in the week to see the space, and taken a bunch of pictures and measurements of all the rooms and windows. She'd suggested that they meet at the Morning Muffin around ten today to review what she'd come up with.

Molly arrived a few minutes early and even though she'd already eaten breakfast with Christian, it was almost four hours ago so she didn't feel too guilty about having a snack. The lemon poppy seed scones looked amazing, so she ordered one along with a half decaf-half hazelnut coffee, and then settled at a roomy round table near the door.

Traci walked in a few minutes later, carrying an oversized sketch book and a pretty Vera Bradley quilted briefcase. Molly waved her over and Traci quickly set her stuff down, then went off to the counter to place her order. She returned a few minutes later with a latte and a toasted sesame bagel with cream cheese.

"I'm so glad we missed the breakfast rush, I'm starving!" Traci took a quick bite of her bagel, then opened her sketchbook and pulled a skinny Mac Air laptop out of her briefcase. Molly was entranced as Traci walked her through her designs and ideas for Rose Cottage. She alternated between showing her delicate drawings of each room, with the overall shape and feel that she had in mind, and actual pictures on the laptop of the colors, fabrics and tiles that she envisioned.

"So, what do you think?" Traci asked nervously, as she closed the sketchbook. Molly hadn't yet said a word, and even realized she'd held her breath once or twice, paying close attention as Traci flipped the pages.

"I'm in love! I'm just so impressed and in awe of what you do. I know what I like when I see it, but I couldn't begin to put it together like this. It's almost as if you read my mind, it's just perfect." The words poured out in a rush, as Molly was just so excited by what Traci had come up with. The colors were soft and welcoming and a bit luxurious. Exactly the feeling you'd want to have when you stayed in an upscale inn.

"I'm so glad," Traci said, and then they discussed prices and timelines, and agreed to get started right away. They chatted a bit longer, had just made arrangements to meet the following Monday to head to the fabric shop Traci favored, when suddenly Traci stopped talking mid-sentence, then leaned in and spoke softly, "Christian's ex just walked in, and it looks like she's heading this way. Have you met her?"

Molly nodded yes, and glanced up as Isabella approached the table. She smiled and spoke first, "Hello Isabella, so nice to see you again." Isabella stopped for a moment, perhaps a bit surprised that Molly had spoken first, but she quickly recovered.

"I understand congratulations are in order," she said smoothly. "It seems like you've made yourself right at home here. Married life must agree with you?" The words were friendly enough, but there was an undercurrent of something else. Molly sympathized though. It couldn't have been easy having your boyfriend ending things so abruptly, and then marrying someone else in a matter of weeks. Molly suspected that although Christian had said it was never serious between them, Isabella might have had a different idea about that.

"So far so good," Molly said, with a polite smile.

"Glad to hear it, and we'll be seeing both of you soon at Daddy's annual barbeque next weekend? I'm sure Christian told you what a big deal it is?" That threw Molly, because it was actually the first she'd heard of it.

"Of course he did," she lied smoothly. "We're both looking forward to it." Traci kicked her under the table, and Molly couldn't look at her until Isabella had safely walked out the door.

"Christian hasn't even mentioned it yet, has he?" Traci commented.

"Was it that obvious?" Molly asked, wondering if Isabella had picked up on her hesitation, as well.

"No, I don't think so. You covered well."

"So what is this barbeque all about? Is it really that big a deal?" And why hadn't Christian mentioned it?

"It is kind of a big deal. Just about everyone in town will be there."

"Are you going?"

"I wouldn't miss it. There's always some kind of drama going on there and it's great for networking."

"Well, at least if you're going, I'll know one person there."

"I'm sure your mother and aunt will be there too."

"Really? Funny that they haven't mentioned it, either."

"I wouldn't be concerned about it. They probably just assume you know about it and are planning to go."

"Right, that must be it." Molly agreed, acting like it was no big deal that her family and husband had failed to mention a huge party thrown by his ex-girlfriend.

Chapter 6

Molly drove straight to her mother and aunt's house after she left the Muffin. She was going to wait to talk to Christian at dinner later. But, until then, she had nothing else pressing to do and the empty hours ahead made her feel antsy and restless. Even if she didn't get answers, at least she could kill time catching up with her mother and aunt.

They were just sitting down to lunch when Molly walked through the door. Her mother looked startled. "Well this is a nice surprise!"

"Perfect timing! We were just about to eat," Aunt Betty chimed in. "Your mother made a big batch of clam chowder; your favorite, if I remember?"

Molly was about to say she wasn't hungry, but then as her stomach rumbled realized she was a bit. Though she'd nibbled on a scone, she and Traci had spent the better part of two hours going over designs. The time had flown.

"I was just in the area, at the Muffin, meeting with Traci about the Rose Cottage decoration," she explained, as her aunt filled a soup bowl generously with creamy chowder, put a dollop of softened butter on top, a shake of paprika and pinch of chopped fresh parsley. Her mother's gift was cooking, and her aunt was all about the show, how the dish was presented. They were quite a team.

Between bites of chowder, she filled them in on the plans for Rose Cottage. After they'd finished and had moved on to tea and slices of Aunt Betty's famous coffee cake, Molly waited until they were happily full and chatting comfortably about what all their friends were up to. Aunt Betty knew everything about everyone it seemed, so it was really all the more curious why neither of them had mentioned Isabella's party.

"So, I hear you're both likely to be going to Isabella's big bash next weekend? Is that true?"

Her mother shot her aunt a look that Molly knew well. Though she didn't say a word, her accusatory glance was crystal clear.

"I didn't say a thing," her aunt protested.

"But why keep it a secret?" Molly asked her mother.

"It's not a secret, as you've probably heard by now; just about everyone we know in town will be likely be there."

"My point exactly," Aunt Betty interjected. "Your mother made me promise not to say anything to you about it, and as you can imagine that hasn't been easy," she said with a chuckle.

"I just didn't want her to say anything until you mentioned it to us. Christian hasn't told you about it yet, has he?"

"No," Molly admitted.

"I figured as much. Honey, he probably just hasn't decided whether or not it's worth the aggravation of going, and wants to spare you any possible awkwardness. Isabella can be a bit unpredictable."

"Not to mention dramatic," Aunt Betty agreed.

"You're probably right," Molly said.

"So, now that she knows, let's discuss what we're going to wear." Aunt Betty and her mother debated their options, while Molly let her mind drift, wondering if her mother was right about Christian's reason for not mentioning the party.

Mrs. O'Brien had the day off, so Molly spent the late afternoon puttering around the kitchen, making a meat sauce and putting a lasagna together. She had just pulled it out of the oven when Christian walked through the door.

His usual routine was to head straight upstairs to change when he was done working for the day, and then join her for dinner in the kitchen. Today, however, he didn't even step into the kitchen, just poked his head in the door and asked, "Want to see something amazing? Mandy's in hard labor. The foal will be here soon, so we need to go quickly."

Molly grabbed a light jacket and followed Christian out the door. The barn where the ranch horses were kept was about a half mile down the road, so they hopped into his Jeep.

"Have you ever seen a live birth before?" Christian asked. His excitement was contagious.

"No, never." Years ago, Molly's family had a cat that gave birth to a litter of kittens, but she'd taken care of it herself, clearing a space in the closet and only making a sound after all six babies were born.

"Mandy's been with us for three years now. She's one of our best work horses. Dr. Jones is on his way, just in case we run into any issues."

They parked and went into the stable, where Mandy was surrounded by several of Christian's men who were keeping her calm, as she seemed agitated.

"How's she doing?" Molly picked up a note of nervousness in Christian's voice.

"About the same," his foreman, Kevin Anderson answered. "Doc coming?"

"He's on his way." Christian walked up to the pretty golden-colored horse, who nuzzled his arm when she saw him and let out a sad whimper.

"I know, baby. It'll be better soon, I promise," he murmured to the horse, as he gently stroked her back and rubbed her neck.

"Something doesn't look right." Henry, one of Christian's most senior men was at Mandy's other end. "You ever deliver a breech before?"

"No, not yet." Christian answered.

"First time for everything. For me too. I've seen quite a few of them, though, over the years. I could probably walk you through it, if need be."

"Hopefully, Doc will be here before then. Should be any time now."

"Okay, but you might want to tell her that. She's starting to push, and that's not good."

Molly watched the scene before her with alarm. The normally sweet tempered horse now looked petrified and in severe pain. She let out a blood-curdling scream that gave Molly goose-bumps and made Christian take a step back.

"You need to get right in there," Henry instructed. "Reach in and shift that baby down, so she can come out smoothly. Kevin and I will hold either side of her."

Christian only hesitated for a second before he stepped forward, rolled his sleeves up as far as they could go and then plunged his hand deep into Mandy.

"It's not working, nothing is moving."

"You gotta keep pulling and pushing until it does," Henry said.

"Okay, I think I'm almost there." It seemed like an eternity, but was only a few minutes before Christian slowly pulled his arm out and, a moment later, with a burst of energy, Mandy dropped her foal. The baby horse lay there motionless until its mother licked its forehead, and then it let out a small sound and slowly moved its legs. Henry explained that the foal would actually be able to stand by itself within an hour or two.

"So, what did you think?" Christian asked proudly.

Molly realized she had tears running down her face. "Amazing."

At that moment, Dr. Jones walked into the stable, sized up the situation, then said, "Looks like you don't need me here." Congratulations were given all around and the doctor checked both animals, pronouncing them healthy and doing well.

"I'm sorry I wasn't able to get here sooner, we ran into some delays at the Ferguson ranch; another breech birth actually. Good to see you've handled that before."

"I have now," Christian said with a grin, "thanks to Henry."

"You did all the work," Henry said gruffly. "I just told you what to do, that's the easy part."

"What happens now?" Molly asked.

"They rest, and we eat."

***

An hour later, a freshly showered Christian joined Molly in the kitchen and they sat down to eat. Over lasagna, salad and garlic bread, Molly filled him in on her meeting with Traci and their plans for Rose Cottage.

"That sounds great! When did she say she could have it done by?"

"The guys said that the physical remodeling should be finished end of this week, and then she'll only need two weeks to do everything. We could be up and running after that."

They discussed plans to get the inn opened. Molly thought her mother and aunt might want to help with the food. Aunt Betty's coffee cake and her mother's chowder would be perfect for a bed and breakfast. They didn't want to run a full restaurant, but Molly thought that being able to offer a light lunch of soup or salad could set them apart from other B-and-Bs, and of course there would be freshly baked cookies and lemonade in the afternoon, and wine and cheese before dinner. Her guests would be on their own for dinner, but she would have menus from the local restaurants available to help them decide.

"You know you may want to talk to Isabella. She could be a good source of referrals for you." Christian's suggestion took her by surprise.

"You think?" Molly wasn't enthused by that idea.

"Sure. Think about it. She regularly meets with people who are thinking about moving to Beauville, and some are going to be from out of town looking for a place to stay while they're here. I bet she gets asked all the time for recommendations."

"I suppose you're right," Molly admitted grudgingly. She hated the thought of asking Isabella for help. That reminded her to ask about the party. It had slipped her mind, with the drama of Mandy giving birth.

"Speaking of Isabella, I actually ran into her this morning and she asked if we were planning to go to her big barbeque next weekend. I told her, of course we'd be there. But I don't remember you mentioning it?"

"Oh that." Christian looked annoyed for a moment. "Honestly, the invitation came a few weeks ago, just after we returned from our honeymoon and, at the time, I just didn't want to deal with seeing Isabella. I know that's not fair, but I thought it might be easier for both of us to skip it."

"Well, too late now. I told her we're going."

Christian took another bite of lasagna and thought for a moment.

"You know, it might actually be a good thing. I can talk to her for you, feel her out about referring people."

"I don't know." Molly hesitated. "Why should she help us? Especially me? I'm not sure how I'd feel about that if I were in her shoes."

"I'm sure she's over it all by now," Christian said confidently. "Isabella's a good person, she'll do the right thing."

Chapter 7

Molly spent the better part of an hour staring at the dresses hanging in her closet, waiting for something to jump out as the obvious choice. But nothing did. Finally, after trying on and rejecting a dozen different options, she reached for an old favorite. It wasn't the most exciting dress, and it was a few years old, but it was the most flattering one she owned. Meghan called it her 'miracle dress' as it was solid black, which made her look a few pounds slimmer, yet it was soft and loose around the waist, so she could relax and eat whatever she liked.

Christian was ready to go when Molly came downstairs. He smiled when he saw her. "You look great!"

"Thanks, you too." Molly couldn't help but admire the way his new jeans hugged his hips and how his navy button-down dress shirt made his blue eyes pop. She wondered if the butterflies in her stomach were just pre-party nerves.

Christian drove, and they arrived at Isabella's family ranch about twenty minutes later. It was just past seven, and there were already hundreds of people there. A huge tent had been set up to accommodate the crowd, and at first there was an overwhelming sea of people as they walked in. Cocktail tables were scattered here and there and, as they headed toward the bar, Christian was stopped repeatedly by people he knew, and introductions were made to those that Molly hadn't yet met, which was about half of them. Finally, as they reached the bar, Molly spotted her mother and aunt at one of the tables. They'd staked out a spot closest to the main bar. Aunt Betty waved them over excitedly, as soon as she saw them.

"How long have you been here?" Molly asked, noticing that their drinks were half-empty.

"Maybe a half-hour," Aunt Betty said.

"Closer to an hour," her mother corrected. "Your aunt wanted to be sure to get a good spot for people-watching."

Christian said a quick hello, and then went to the bar to get a round of drinks for everyone.

"Have you seen her?" Aunt Betty asked.

"Isabella? No, surprisingly we haven't run into her yet."

"She must be in the main house, probably checking with the caterers." Aunt Betty said, as a server carrying an elegant tray of stuffed mushrooms came by. They each took one and Molly grabbed an extra for Christian. He returned a minute later with everyone's drinks. Molly took a sip of Chardonnay and surveyed the room. There had to be at least three hundred people here, and although most of them were strangers, she was pleased to see that she recognized quite a few of them. Just about everyone who had attended their wedding was here, as well as other friends of her mother and aunt that she'd met recently.

"I told you it was quite a scene," Aunt Betty said, as she accepted another *hors d'oeuvre*, this time *spanakopita*, a delicious triangle of puff pastry wrapped around a filling of spinach and cheese.

"Don't forget there's a massive buffet coming," her mother said, as Aunt Betty reached for a second *spanakopita*.

"Do you mind if I take off for a bit? There's a few people I need to talk to." Christian was being waved down by three men at another table.

"Of course not." Molly recognized the men as local contractors and also members of the men's golf league that Christian played in every Wednesday night. They were at a table at the edge of the crowd, drinking whiskey on the rocks and smoking cigars.

"Your Christian looks very handsome tonight." Aunt Betty had a matchmaking gleam in her eye. Molly didn't want them to get any false hopes.

"He does," she agreed. "But he's only 'my Christian' for six months."

"We'll see." Aunt Betty then turned her attention to the crowd and kept them in stitches for the next twenty minutes or so. She knew something about everyone that passed by their table, and some of it was so outrageous that Molly thought she was making it up.

"That's Phil Thompson," her aunt said, as an elderly gentleman with snow white hair stopped by Christian's table to say hello.

"He's in his early nineties, just lost his wife a year ago, and has now turned into a social butterfly. Even has a Facebook page. Says it keeps him young. He still drives, has two convertibles, one of which he painted himself with leftover boat paint. He's the guy with the smiley face car."

Molly smiled, as she pictured the car. She'd seen it a few times around town. It was a small older-model Capri, painted a pale green color, with a giant yellow and black smiley face on each door. She hadn't yet met Mr. Thompson, but had a feeling she was going to like him.

Christian returned to their table a few minutes later with Mr. Thompson by his side, and introduced Molly to him.

"I'm so sorry I had to miss your wedding. I heard it was really something. I had a little mishap that slowed me down a bit. Damn hospital insisted on keeping me for three nights. Can you imagine? They wanted me to stay longer, but I'd had enough and checked myself out."

"I hope you're feeling better," Molly said.

"I was never sick, young lady. Not for a minute. I just needed a new ladder. I was outside painting and my ladder gave way. They thought I'd broken my hip or something, but it was just a bad sprain. My daughter gave me hell though. Made me promise to stay off ladders. Told her I would, but we'll see."

They chatted with the lively Mr. Thompson for a bit longer, until he was spotted by two older ladies who waved him over to their table.

"Oh, I'm in for it now," he said, with a gleam in his eye. "So many pretty ladies, so little time." With that, he left them and Christian added, "He was one of my grandfather's best friends. He's all talk, you know. His wife, Ellen, was the love of his life. This past year has been really tough for him. He's just starting to get out and about now."

"I hope I have half his energy when I get to his age."

"I wish I had his energy now!" Isabella exclaimed. She'd suddenly appeared at their table and welcomed them all. They all chatted for a few minutes, and then Isabella was ready to move on.

"They are bringing out the food now. Be sure to help yourself when you're ready. Daddy's barbeque sauce is legendary. Oh, and Molly, I love your dress." Molly couldn't tell from her tone if she meant it. It kind of reminded her of the sugar-sweet Southern comment 'Bless her heart', which meant anything but.

"Thanks, yours is amazing," Molly responded. She actually felt a bit like a plain Jane though, standing next to Isabella. *Her* dress was really something. It was an elegant cream shade and of a stretchy jersey-like material that showed off her near perfect hourglass figure. It was very Marilyn Monroe, with a skirt that flowed out just below the knees and a sexy halter top with pearl beading on the bodice. Her hair was done to perfection, in a carefully curled tangle of loose spirals that were gathered up at the sides and fell dramatically down her back. Her cowboy boots were gorgeous too; the heels were so high that Molly wondered how she managed walking in them. But she did, and they caused her hips to swing confidently back and forth as she walked away, knowing that the attention of most of the men nearby was on her.

Including Christian, who started to walk after her. "I forgot to ask her about the inn referrals. Be right back."

He caught up to her easily, as she wasn't moving too quickly in those heels. They were just far enough away that Molly couldn't hear the conversation, but it didn't look like it was going well. Isabella was all smiles when Christian first caught up to her, but within a few minutes her face took on a stormy look and she ended the conversation abruptly, turning around and walking away while Christian was still talking. A few moments later, he returned to the table looking a bit confused.

"I take it she didn't love your suggestion?" Molly asked.

"I think she'll come around," he said and then, when Molly raised her eyebrow at that, he added, "eventually. I think I just caught her off-guard. She's busy with the party right now. She asked me if I was kidding, and then said we'd discuss this at another time."

"What did you ask her?" Aunt Betty was dying to know, and Molly could see the curiosity on her mom's face as well. She hadn't yet mentioned Christian's idea to them, so she quickly filled them in. When she finished, Aunt Betty gave Christian a smack on the arm.

"What on earth were you thinking? You asked your ex-girlfriend to refer people to your new wife's business venture, less than a month after you broke up?"

Christian looked surprised. "I guess it wasn't the best idea. I really thought she wouldn't mind, since she knows the details behind our marriage."

"All she knows is that you're with someone else now," Aunt Betty said.

"The buffet is open, anyone ready to head over?" her mother asked. Molly knew it as an attempt to change the subject.

"I'm ready and starving, let's go."

The amount of food was staggering: several different kinds of meats and barbeque sauces; all kinds of side dishes, most involving butter, cream and cheese, veggies, salads, and hot, crusty rolls. They all piled their plates and raved about the food.

Isabella's father had cooked the meats, but they'd used a caterer for everything else. Molly made a note to find out the name of the caterer and keep them in mind, if they ever needed to use one at the inn.

While they were eating, a jazz band played softly in the background. When they were just about finished, a different band came on, and started playing livelier dance tunes. By the second song, people were making their way onto the makeshift dance floor. Molly excused herself to hit the ladies room, and just as she was about to exit the stall she heard a familiar voice and paused.

"He actually asked me to give referrals to his new wife. To help her. Can you believe it?" Isabella sounded furious, and Molly decided to wait a moment or two longer, hoping Isabella and her confidant would leave.

"Men are so dumb. Completely clueless. I bet it didn't even occur to him that the suggestion was completely inappropriate." Molly didn't recognize the other voice, but it sounded like it was coming from an older woman, possibly Isabella's mother.

"I told him we'd talk about it later, just to get rid of him. There's really nothing to talk about, though. How could imagine that I would possibly help her, of all people?"

Molly cringed at that. Isabella clearly had no interest in being her friend. She actually sounded like she hated her, and given the situation, she supposed she couldn't really blame her. She didn't want to further embarrass her by walking out now, so she stayed put and was relieved when she heard them leave a moment later.

She was drying her hands, when Isabella walked back into the bathroom and stopped in her tracks when she saw Molly. Molly could see the wheels turning, as she was wondering if she'd heard her talking.

Isabella spotted a lipstick by the mirror and snatched it up.

"I just realized I left this behind."

Molly hesitated for a second. She wanted to apologize, but then it would be clear to Isabella that she'd overheard her conversation. So, instead, she simply said, "Thank you so much for inviting us. Dinner was wonderful."

"Christian is always invited," Isabella snapped, then added a bit more graciously, "I'm glad you are enjoying yourself. If you'll excuse me, I have to get back to my guests." Without waiting for a response she was gone, and Molly wondered if despite his good intentions Christian had actually made matters worse. Isabella was in a position to not only help them, but she could also do some damage if she wanted to, by steering people away from Rose Cottage. Molly felt guilty for a moment for letting her thoughts go in that direction. Isabella wasn't happy to be dumped, who would be? But Molly couldn't imagine that she'd be that vindictive. Christian was probably right, and she was just taken off guard. Although Molly wasn't counting on a referral any time soon.

***

The following week flew by. Christian was busier than usual, dealing with day-to-day ranch issues, as well as on the real estate development side, putting finishing touches on several houses that were almost ready to hit the market. Meanwhile Molly was spending most of her time at Rose Cottage, working closely with Traci on the decorating which, to her delight, Traci actually completed late Friday afternoon, ahead of schedule. To celebrate, Molly impulsively invited her out to the ranch that evening for dinner and drinks, and told her to bring Travis along, if he'd like to join them. She knew Christian would enjoy hanging out with his best friend.

She called Christian to give him the heads-up on her way back to the ranch, and stopped by the local market to pick up some wine and cheese to have with dinner. A little later, Molly came downstairs after showering and blow-drying her hair and was on her way into the kitchen to start prepping for dinner, when she saw something out of the corner of her eye that made her stop and take a step backwards for another look. Christian was in his office, sitting in his favorite leather chair, head back and mouth wide open. He was sound asleep, with Toby curled up by his feet.

Molly hated to disturb him, but she needed to wake him up so he could jump in the shower and get ready before their guests arrived. She walked over, gently touched his shoulder and his eyes flew open.

"Sorry, you looked so comfortable, but Travis and Traci will be here in about a half hour."

Christian looked confused for a moment, then rubbed his eyes and leaned forward.

"Thanks. I can't believe I conked out like that."

"Long day?" Molly knew it had been. She'd hardly talked to Christian all week, except for a few minutes at breakfast and dinner when he'd filled her in on what was going on at work, and she'd updated him on the progress at the Rose Cottage. He'd gone straight into his home office after dinner every night to get caught up on paperwork, and then had fallen asleep on the sofa most nights before eight.

"Yeah, but it's all good, it's Friday now. I'll catch a second wind in the shower and see you soon. Thanks for taking care of dinner." He smiled and laugh lines lit up his face. The stress of the week seemed to be falling away, and Molly was glad to see it.

"I'm happy to do it, it's fun for me. Hopefully they both like seafood. We're having shrimp scampi."

"They'll love it." Christian slowly got to his feet and went upstairs to shower, while Molly started puttering around the kitchen. A half hour later, the doorbell rang just as Christian was coming down the stairs, looking decidedly more awake after a shower and shave. He opened the door and Traci and Travis came in. Traci handed Molly a chilled bottle of Pinot Grigio and Travis passed over a six-pack of beer—an IPA from a local brewery—to Christian, who took two out and put the rest in the refrigerator. Molly poured glasses of wine for Traci and herself.

One of the things Molly loved about Christian's house was his kitchen. Although he rarely cooked, it was set up beautifully for anyone who enjoyed entertaining. It wasn't an overly large kitchen, but rather the perfect size, with just the right amount of room between the refrigerator, stove, sink and island, so that Molly was just a step or two away from whatever she needed. Her favorite feature was the beautiful Carerra marble island that was crisp white with soft streaks of gray throughout. She loved the smooth feel of the honed marble, and that it was V-shaped with a gas stove in the middle and raised countertops with three stools on each side, so that while she was cooking, she could face her guests and chat easily.

She'd set out a platter of assorted cheeses and crackers a few minutes before they arrived, and as soon as everyone was settled around the island, they dug in.

"What's this one? Looks interesting." Molly liked to have a mix of cheeses, and tonight she'd chosen a few familiar favorites: a creamy aged cheddar; a mild and nutty manchego that was great for nibbling; St. Andre, which was a soft, buttery triple cream; and the one that Traci was asking about, which was a white pie-like wedge with a gray ashy line in the middle.

"That's Humboldt Fog. It's an aged goat cheese, soft and like brie around the edge, a little sharper in the middle. The gray ash-like stuff is all edible." Molly had discovered this cheese a few years ago, when a local cheese shop in Manhattan had come into the hotel and done a tasting for the chef and staff. She'd been a fan of it ever since.

Traci took a small amount of the cheese, spread it on a cracker and took a bite. "It's amazing." Molly smiled at the look of pure bliss on her face.

The four of them chatted easily, while Molly finished up cooking. She'd done most of the prep work earlier: the salad was all assembled except for the walnuts, which were in the oven toasting while the pasta was cooking.

The shrimp scampi came together quickly, as she added a generous amount of butter to a sauté pan, followed by a splash of good olive oil, some garlic and chopped tomatoes. She gave that about a minute, then added a generous helping of the wine that Traci had brought, let it reduce down a little, then added the shrimp. They only needed a few minutes, and during that time she took the walnuts out of the oven and added them to the salad which also had dried cranberries and goat cheese. She tossed it all together with some balsamic dressing and the heat of the nuts worked a bit of magic with the goat cheese, melting it just enough to add a delicious creaminess to the salad.

The last step was to drain the pasta, swirl in a bit more butter and a squeeze of lemon on the scampi, and then plate it up for everyone with a sprinkle of chopped parsley on top. They relocated from the island bar to the round wooden table by a gas fireplace that divided the kitchen and family room.

Everyone raved about the scampi and the salad. Molly was pleased. She loved to cook, and had actually learned how to make the scampi by watching the cooks at the hotel and asking questions every now and then. They'd got a kick out of it and whenever it had been slow, they'd taken turns in showing her how they did different things, such as adding wine to a pan that had been used to brown chicken or steak and letting it reduce down to make a delicious sauce by scraping up the bits on the bottom.

"You know, I have an idea," Traci began. "I know you aren't planning to have a full restaurant, but what about doing an occasional wine dinner? That might be a way to draw new people in, something extra you could offer."

"You'd need to get a liquor license if you're going to serve alcohol," said Travis, always the lawyer. "I'm pretty tight with the guys on the licensing board. It might not be that difficult if we just go for beer and wine and a catering license versus bar."

Molly loved the idea. "We can see if the catering company that did Isabella's party might be interested."

"Or you could cook." Traci said, and looked as though she meant it.

"You could actually. This is a restaurant quality meal." Travis said, as he reached for another helping of salad.

"Would you want to cook though?" Christian asked.

"Honestly, I don't know. I'm flattered that you think I could." Molly had fantasized every now and then about what it would be like to be a caterer. But having seen the craziness at the hotel whenever there was a big function going on had always made her reconsider. Catering was stressful and a lot of hard work. But, on a smaller scale, like an intimate wine dinner at Rose Cottage, she had to admit the idea was intriguing.

Christian helped her clear the plates when they finished eating. Twice while going from the table to the sink, her bare arm accidentally brushed against his and each time the contact generated a spark that surprised her. They'd settled comfortably into the friend space, so this reaction was unexpected. She glanced at Christian's face to see if he was feeling it too, but she couldn't tell. Maybe it was the wine; she'd just poured herself a second glass and was feeling very relaxed and full from dinner.

Chapter 8

Once everything was cleared, Christian and Travis went into the office to enjoy an after dinner drink, while Molly poured cups of coffee for herself and Traci and then took them into the family room to watch a little TV. Christian poured two small glasses of one of his better scotches, and he and Travis settled into the leather chairs by the fireplace. Christian had lit the fire earlier and though it was dying down now, it still threw a little heat and cast a warm glow on the room. Toby approved and flopped down between the two of them, close enough that he could feel the warmth of the fire on his back.

"We should be keeping you busy over the next month or so as the Harrison Boulevard houses sell," Christian said. Travis handled all of their real estate closings.

"No kidding, that's good to hear." They chatted a bit about the real estate market and upcoming projects, and then Travis changed the subject. "So, how is it going with Molly? You guys look good together. If I didn't know differently, I'd think it was the real deal."

"It's going well enough, better than expected really, considering the circumstances. We've always been good friends. Molly is easy to be around."

"You were friends when you were kids. Maybe you could be more? Just saying. You seem good together." Travis was quiet for a moment, then added, "Unless you're not attracted to her?"

"Molly's a beautiful girl," Christian said. He took another sip of scotch and stared at the fire. "It's not that I'm not attracted to her, of course I am. This just isn't a normal situation. Molly's not just any girl. I like her."

"You like her, she's beautiful, so what's the problem?" Travis said reasonably.

"The problem is, I like her too much. We get along great. But you know my history." Christian could only envision things ending badly, and he liked Molly and her family too much to risk that. But still, he had to admit he was surprised by how much he liked having her around, and by how attracted he really was to her. It scared him a little. He hadn't felt this level of interest since Heather Olander, the fiancée who'd dumped him out of the blue. He frowned and took a sip of his scotch. Definitely best not to even go there; easier for everyone in the long run.

"So you got burned once, and now have it in your mind that you'll never be serious with anyone, never commit or get married. How's that working out for you?" Travis challenged him.

"It's fine; everything was fine until Gramps lost his mind and changed his will."

"Really? You honestly think everything was fine? You think Isabella was happy with how things were? That she didn't want more? Most people want more."

"She seemed happy."

"Maybe she was, but maybe she also thought you'd come around eventually."

"I was always honest with her."

"Yes, but are you being honest with yourself? How do you really feel about Molly?" Travis paused to take a sip of scotch, was quiet for a moment then said, "Maybe your grandfather was smarter than you realize. Why not use this time to see if she might be the one?"

"It's not that simple. She has a life across the country to return to: a career she loves, and the promotion she's been working towards is almost there. It could never work." They sat in silence for a few minutes, sipping their scotch and enjoying the warmth of the fire.

"It might not work." Travis finally agreed, "But how will you know, if you never try? Things change, people change."

Christian said nothing to that, just took another sip of scotch, and then reached over to scratch Toby behind his ears.

"Speaking of Isabella," Travis went on, changing the subject again. "I picked up a message from her on the way over here. She is going to stop by the office tomorrow morning. She has something she needs help with."

"Probably another closing," Christian said. Isabella also often used Travis for her many real estate transactions.

"I was thinking about asking her out to dinner. You sure you're still cool with that?" There was a hint of nervousness in Travis's voice, and Christian realized his friend had it bad. Normally neither of them would ever consider dating an exgirlfriend, but this was different. Christian thought the world of both of them and now understood why Travis was being so insistent about Molly.

"Totally cool with it." Christian assured him.

After Travis and Traci had left, Molly decided to call it a night too. She took her coffee cup into the kitchen, rinsed and put it in the dishwasher, and then poured herself a glass of water to take up to bed. She rarely drank the water, but always had a glass by her bedside in case she woke up thirsty. She was about to head to bed when, suddenly, Christian appeared, and had a worried look as though he needed to talk to her about something.

"Everything all right?" she asked.

"What?" He seemed surprised by the question, as he leaned against the kitchen counter and glanced around the room, looking everywhere except at Molly.

"You seem concerned about something, or distracted, not sure which." Maybe he was just exhausted, a little off after the long week.

"Are you staying up for a while?"

Molly hesitated, then said, "I was thinking of heading to bed, but I could stay up for a bit." She wasn't tired anymore, as there was an interesting shift of energy in the room. The slight spark she'd felt when she and Christian had accidentally brushed against each other was back, and they hadn't even touched this time.

"Good, I thought I'd show you the plans for the new project we're breaking ground on next week." He sounded excited and a bit nervous, and Molly wasn't sure what to think as he led her into the office and pulled out a huge poster board and laid it on top of his desk.

"This is going to be a high-end market, in the middle of the Brookstone development. It will have the best meats, cheeses, local produce and a smaller version of the Community Co-op, with an attached liquor and wine shop."

"That's a wonderful idea!" Molly knew it would be a hit. The closest Community Co-op, with its huge selection of organic and prepared foods, was in Bozeman. Molly had a little trouble concentrating as Christian walked her through the plans. He was standing so close to her that his arm brushed against her each time he leaned forward to point something out. Molly leaned a little closer, liking the feeling of being so near him.

"Thanks! Your support means a lot to me." He gave her a quick hug, and Molly held on tight, loving the smell of him. It wasn't any particular cologne, just the mix of shampoo and his natural scent. When they pulled apart, his eyes locked on hers and she held his glance, and her breath, as she could sense what was coming next. Christian moved towards her, hesitated a moment and then his lips were on hers.

Molly held on tighter as Christian deepened the kiss. Then he pulled back and slowly kissed his way along her neck, before claiming her lips again. Molly reveled in the taste of him and wasn't surprised at the chemistry; the surges of electricity she'd been feeling whenever they touched made sense now. She didn't want the kiss to end, but eventually it did, as Christian pulled back and then gently kissed her forehead.

"I shouldn't have done that," he said.

"I didn't mind actually." Molly smiled up at him, but the warm and happy glow she'd been feeling was starting to fade at the look of obvious regret on Christian's face.

"It's not fair to you. I'll make sure it doesn't happen again." Christian turned away and started heading upstairs to bed, while Molly stayed in the kitchen, wide awake and wondering where they would go from here, and how she could get Christian to kiss her again.

Chapter 9

The next morning at breakfast, Christian acted as though the kiss had never happened. He wasn't distant, just overly polite and friendly, almost as if he was trying too hard. Molly just went with it and, within a few days, it was almost as if they were back to normal. Though Molly did find herself glancing his way more often, and a few times out of the corner of her eye she caught him doing the same. She had of course filled Meghan in about the kiss, and they'd had a good hour-long phone chat about the matter.

Meghan had ridden the roller coaster of emotions, from initially thrilled for her to wondering how it could possibly work because Molly was absolutely without a doubt coming back to New York, right? Molly had assured her that she was planning on it and counting on her promotion.

And Christian certainly wasn't leaving Montana. So where did that leave them? As attracted as she was to Christian, she had to admit there wasn't likely to be a future there. And at least he was decent enough to recognize it too and stop, before things got out of hand. But still, if Molly was being honest with herself, she couldn't help wondering what it would be like if they just gave in and enjoyed themselves. After all they were married; what would be the harm in it if they both went into it with their eyes open? Enjoyed the rest of their time together? The idea was a bit scandalous, as she'd never been one for casual affairs. But it certainly was tempting. But who was she kidding: if she'd never been one for a casual 'friends with benefits' arrangement, she certainly wasn't going to start now. No, somewhat regretfully, she recognized that she was an all or nothing kind of girl. The complete opposite of what Christian wanted.

She didn't have much time to dwell on it, though, as the rest of the week flew by. Molly, her mother and aunt were non-stop busy as they finished up getting the Rose Cottage ready for its grand opening. Traci and Molly had chosen soft lilac and pale green colors for the walls and drapes, and classic snow white linens. Soothing gray throw pillows added the final touch. Aunt Betty found some amazing inexpensive watercolors, and they hung different ones in each room and in the hallways to add a burst of welcoming color.

They also made sure that all the bathrooms were stocked with high end soaps and shampoos. Molly's mother had a knack for decorating as well, and added finishing touches to all the rooms, such as whimsical bubble bath, pretty dried flower arrangements and interesting magazines and books. She also came up with an idea that Molly fell in love with: to leave a pair of signature socks in the room for every guest. Some high end hotels offered slippers, so they would differentiate themselves by offering soft cozy socks in stripes of the inn's colors: lilac, mint, and gray.

To celebrate the opening, they had decided to have people over for a 'breakfast at dinner' reception that Thursday evening, with the inn officially opening for business the following day. Molly worked closely with her mother and aunt on the guest list of about one hundred people. A few were close friends, but the majority were business people who would be in a position of influence, such as Isabella, her caterer, as well as other local realtors, attorneys and the owners of Delancey's and the Morning Muffin.

Molly even invited the owners of the small motel they'd passed on the way into town. Although they could technically be considered competition, strategically she thought it made sense to get to know them, as there were bound to be times when they'd have no vacancies and would need to refer people to each other.

They kept the menu for the opening simple, and decided to feature food they planned to serve at the inn, such as her mother's legendary caramelized onion and mushroom quiche; a puff pastry tart with fig jam; *prosciutto*; goat cheese and arugula; chicken apple sausage; lemon ginger scones; Aunt Betty's cinnamon walnut coffee cake; and fresh baked chocolate chip cookies. They also put out a platter of assorted cheeses and crackers for guests to nibble on as they arrived and a tray of mimosas made with freshly squeezed orange juice, as well as carafes of the red and white wines they intended to offer.

So it was a somewhat casual and informal affair that immediately put people at ease. Molly also had two local girls helping out. They kept the carafes of wine full and served the *hors d'oeuvres*, which were bite-sized portions of everything.

Their first guests arrived a few minutes past six. Although Molly had been a bundle of nerves all day as they got ready for the party, an hour later, once most of the guests were there and everything seemed to be going well, she felt herself finally start to relax.

"Here, you deserve some wine now," Aunt Betty said, as she passed Molly a freshly poured glass of Malbec. Molly had been so busy running around making sure all her guests were taken care of, that she hadn't had anything to eat or drink herself.

She'd just taken her first sip when she saw another guest arrive. Isabella certainly knew how to make an entrance. She was wearing a fire engine red denim dress that hugged her curves and looked amazing against her dark hair. Molly was surprised to see that Travis was by her side. She wondered if that was a coincidence, or if they'd come together.

Travis immediately made his way over to Christian, who was helping himself to the cheese and crackers.

"You made it finally," he said, as he saw Travis. "Red wine?" Travis nodded and Christian handed him a glass. It wasn't like Travis to be so late to a party; he was usually the first one there.

"Sorry, got stuck working late. Isabella had to reschedule her meeting with me until the end of day. We just finished up and came right over."

"Everything go okay?" Travis seemed a bit tense, not his usual easy-going self.

"It wasn't quite what I expected. Can't say more than that due to confidentiality, but you'll probably know what I'm talking about soon enough."

"Oh, okay..." Then to lighten the mood, Christian added, "So, did you ask Isabella out then? You said you were going to, when she came by the office."

Travis hesitated then said, "I did say that, didn't I? I decided to put that idea on hold; there's no reason to rush." Christian found that odd and very un-like Travis, but it was clear that his friend wasn't going to share anything further, so he changed the subject.

"We got a verbal agreement on another offer. I should be calling you tomorrow to confirm date for the P-and-S."

"That's great." Travis looked more relaxed now as they started to discuss the terms of the offer. While they talked, Christian automatically scanned the room, looking for Molly. She was handing out mimosas to two friends of her mother, and hadn't stopped moving since the party began. Isabella was standing nearby, chatting with a few other realtors. Christian couldn't help but compare the two. Isabella stood out in the crowd with her bright dress and dramatic coloring, but it was Molly that his eyes lingered over.

She was wearing a shimmery soft lilac dress that was pure elegance. Her hair was twisted into a smooth French twist, with a few wisps left loose to frame either side of her face. She smiled often, as she walked around the room chatting with everyone and making them feel welcome, and Christian had to fight the urge to pull her into a side room and have her all to himself.

It had been a difficult week, trying to act as though that kiss hadn't happened, and that they were just good friends. As much as he enjoyed her company, he couldn't be around her now without wanting to kiss her again, so the easiest thing was to just spend less time together.

"Christian, could I have a word with you?" Isabella had walked up to them and he hadn't even seen her coming. Travis immediately looked uncomfortable.

"I see a few people I need to say hello to." Travis quickly walked away, leaving the two of them alone.

"How've you been?" Isabella asked sweetly.

"Good, thanks. You?"

"Never better." She took a sip of her wine, glanced around the room for a moment, then continued, "So, I thought I should let you know that I won't be able to send referrals your way."

"No? I'm sorry to hear that."

"I thought it best to tell you the news myself, rather than have you hear it from someone else."

"Okay." Christian was starting to feel irritated; as usual Isabella tended to be overly dramatic. "It's not that big a deal; if you're not comfortable referring people, I guess I understand."

"No, it's not that. The thing is I can't refer people to Rose Cottage, because I'm going to be opening a bed and breakfast myself! My great uncle and I, that is. He wants to move to a smaller, single floor house closer to town. It was his idea actually. He thinks there's plenty of business to go around, and has that big old house with two floors that aren't even being used."

Isabella running a bed and breakfast...Christian couldn't see it.

"What do you know about the hospitality business? It seems like a lot of work running an inn." Christian wondered how Molly would feel about this news, and realized he had to be the one to tell her, tonight.

"You just put people in pretty rooms and serve them muffins and coffee in the morning, how hard can it be?" Isabella said with a dismissive laugh. "I think it's going to be fun!"

Christian seemed preoccupied on the drive home, and was quieter than usual. Molly didn't mind; the party had gone well, but now that it was over she was exhausted. Her energy had crashed after being 'on' all night, making sure everything went well and that everyone was having a good time. It had been nearly ten o'clock by the time they'd cleaned up after everyone had left, and she was looking forward to falling into bed and getting a good night's sleep before their big grand opening day.

As soon as they got home, Molly went straight into the kitchen to pour herself a glass of water and then head to bed, but Christian followed her and said, "Can we talk for a minute?"

"Sure, what's up?" He looked so serious and a bit annoyed, as he dragged his hand through his hair, a habit she'd noticed he had when he was trying to work out a solution to a problem.

"It's Isabella." He then told her about her plans and that it was her great-uncle's idea, the lively Mr. Thompson they'd met at the barbeque.

Molly's initial reaction was shock, followed by amusement, and then finished with annoyance. She found it hard to imagine the always immaculate Isabella cleaning a toilet or changing sheets or even cooking, for that matter.

"Has she ever done anything like this before? Worked in a hotel or bed and breakfast, ever?"

Christian confirmed that she hadn't. "She thinks there's nothing to it."

That's where Molly's feeling of amusement came in. Isabella had no idea what she was in for. But, then annoyance took over again, as she realized this could put a serious wrinkle in their promotion plans. Although she agreed with Mr. Thompson's enthusiasm and belief that the town could support two bed and breakfasts, it still meant that people would have a choice, and Isabella had a lot of influence in town and the ability to make things more difficult than they needed to be.

"Well, looks like we'll have to ramp up our marketing and promotion efforts." They did have a little time before Isabella would be able to open, Christian said she was still a good two months away from being ready. A lot could happen in that time period, and Molly intended to make sure they got off to a great start.

Chapter 10

Their first guests were due to arrive any time after 2pm. Molly, her mother and aunt arrived at Rose Cottage at about 11am. They made sure that all the rooms were ready, pillows fluffed, shades opened to make sure the natural light streamed in and the perfect jazz CD selected for soft background music in the lobby. They only had two rooms booked for tonight, but both parties were staying through the weekend and Molly was actually glad that they weren't full. Having just a few rooms let was ideal, as it would give them a chance to work the kinks out and make sure everything went smoothly.

That morning and for the past week, Molly had had the inn's main number forwarded to her cell phone, so that callers would be sure to reach a live person. As of tomorrow, she'd be at the inn early to greet the guests for breakfast, and she had an answering service lined up for after hours. If there was any kind of emergency at the inn, the service would call her and she'd be able to run right over if need be.

Surprisingly, they'd had quite a few calls in the week before the inn was officially opened, with people wanting to reserve rooms or just ask questions about rates and availability. The website and PR releases she had sent to the local papers, as well as her mother and aunt telling everyone they knew, had all done a great job in getting the word out. Her mom and Betty had insisted on helping Molly out at the inn, by baking and filling in as needed. Today they'd be staying the entire time, to keep her company and see how everything was supposed to go. Though the beginning of next week was slow, they were already almost completely booked from the following Wednesday through the weekend, and Molly was hopeful that they weren't just getting curiosity visitors, but rather this was a sign that they were meeting a real need and things would only get better.

After a quick vacuum of the main hallways and lobby that wasn't really necessary, but that made everyone feel better, they sat down to have lunch in the kitchen. Molly's mother had brought Maine lobster rolls and potato salad, as a special treat to celebrate and bring them luck on opening day. While they were eating, Molly filled them in on Isabella's plans, and Aunt Betty didn't hesitate to voice her opinion on the matter.

"Who does she think she is? That's the most absurd thing I've ever heard." Molly reminded her that supposedly it wasn't Isabella's idea.

"Phil Thompson should know better. I think he's going a bit daffy. Do you know he told me the other day? That he wants to put smiley faces on his truck too? Said he likes the attention he gets."

"Phil's sharp as a tack, and you know it," Molly's mother said, as she helped herself to more potato salad.

"Well, now I know what people were buzzing about this morning at the Muffin. We were there having our coffee, and Isabella was making the rounds a bit more than usual. I didn't think anything of it at the time, figured they were talking about her outfit. I don't think I've ever seen that girl in the same thing twice. She had new shoes on too. Don't know how she manages to walk in those things; the heels must have been at least four inches."

"Molly doesn't have anything to worry about," her mother said matter-of-factly, and Molly smiled back at her. Nothing ever really ruffled her mom, and it was one of the things she admired most about her.

"Thanks. I'm not worried, more like a little irritated. If she chooses to, Isabella could be a nuisance once she opens and starts steering people her way."

"That's true," Aunt Betty agreed. "She's certainly not shy."

"Honey, all you can really focus on is doing a great job here, so people start to spread the word. Remember, you know how to do this and you do it really well." Her mother gave her arm a pat, and then stood up to start clearing the plates.

Once the dishes were taken care of, Molly mixed up a batch of chocolate chip cookie dough and popped a tray of walnut sized balls in the oven at a little past 1:30 pm. That way, the welcoming smell of baking would greet their guests as they arrived and the cookies would still be warm. Aunt Betty mixed up a pitcher of fresh lemonade and, once that was ready, they set it on a long side table in the lobby. When the cookies were done, Molly set a platter full of them by the lemonade, and also put a guest book out so people could sign in and leave comments when they checked out.

Precisely at 2, the front door opened and an older couple in their sixties came in. Molly guessed that they were the Browns. They had told her on the phone when they'd made their reservation that they were coming to Beauville to visit their relatives at a family reunion. After they checked in and Molly gave them their room key, she encouraged them to help themselves to the cookies and lemonade.

"There are menus of our local restaurants over there as well, and please join us for pre-dinner cocktail hour. We'll have several different wines and cheeses available."

"That sounds wonderful, dear," Mrs. Brown said. "We will definitely see you back down here then. We're meeting the relatives for dinner, and a glass of wine before we go sounds perfect."

Within minutes of the Browns departing the lobby, the front door opened again and their other party arrived. The Fergusons were a much younger couple, closer to thirty, Molly guessed. While Joe Ferguson gave Molly his credit card to check in, his wife Emily dived onto the chocolate chip cookies, inhaling one and then bringing a plate with several more back to her husband.

"These are amazing," she said to Molly. "Thank you so much! You have no idea how hungry I am. We've been driving for hours."

"We're in town for the weekend to look at houses," Joe explained.

"He just got a great new job here," Emily said proudly.

"I'm supposed to start in a month, so we need to move fast. Our realtor says she has a great lineup for us to look at, so hopefully everything will work out."

"Who's your realtor?" Molly couldn't help asking.

"Isabella Graham, do you know her?" Of course it was Isabella. Why did she even ask?

"She's very good at what she does. I'm sure she'll take excellent care of you." Molly said, and then invited them to stop by later for wine and cheese.

"This is so great!" Emily said, as she started on her third cookie. "We will see you soon." Molly handed them their key and they headed to their room.

Now that their guests were all set, Molly's mother and aunt got busy in the kitchen, making a caramelized onion and wild mushroom quiche and a walnut coffee cake. Once baked, and then cooled, they put the quiche in the refrigerator so that Molly would be able to quickly heat it up the next day. She was also planning to cut some fresh fruit when she arrived in the morning, and put out a few cold cereals and bagels, so there would be a nice assortment of options.

At about 4:20, Molly set out several bottles of wine, a nice red blend, and a smooth Pinot Grigio that she set in a pretty ice bucket to keep it chilled. For cheeses, she went with a smooth cheddar and a fluffy, mild goat's cheese, along with some crisp rosemary and olive oil crackers. She had decided to make 4:30 the official starting time for cocktail hour, figuring that if her guests were heading out somewhere for dinner they would have plenty of time to get there, especially if their preference was to eat early.

So, she wasn't surprised when, at 4:30 on the dot, the Browns walked into the lobby, followed soon after by the Fergusons. She directed everyone to help themselves. Once they were all set, Molly poured half-glasses of wine for her mother, aunt and herself, and they chatted with their guests for a while, before Molly excused herself to take a call. A few minutes later her mother and Aunt joined her in the kitchen, put their glasses in the dishwasher, and then said their good-byes. Once they left, Molly settled on one of the padded stools at the island, pulled out her laptop and was thrilled to discover that another online reservation had come in, for Monday, so now they wouldn't be completely vacant on any day next week.

She checked on everyone a little later and the lobby was empty. They'd evidently all left for dinner, so she put the cheese and crackers and wine away and then got ready to go home herself. She left a note at the front desk for her guests to call if they needed her, and then grabbed her purse and headed to her car to drive home.

But she didn't get very far. When she turned the key, her engine made an awful clicking sound. She tried a few more times to no avail, and then called Christian, who said he'd be right over. Though it was still light outside, the air was bone chillingly cold, so Molly scurried back inside to wait in the warmth.

She opened her laptop back up again to kill time while she waited for Christian to arrive, and although she'd checked the reservations calendar several times that day, she clicked on it again and checked her email once more. A query had come in, asking about availability for the following week, and Molly was typing up a reply as Christian walked in.

Molly smiled as she saw him, and said, "Thanks so much. Sorry to be a bother." Christian's hair was still a bit damp, and

Molly knew he'd likely just taken his after-work shower. It was the first thing he usually did when he got home if he'd spent much time outside, which was often.

"Don't be silly, it's no bother. How did it go today?" Christian leaned against the kitchen island and glanced at the laptop. Molly had just hit send, which brought up the reservations screen.

"Are those the current reservations?" He asked.

"Yes, we've had quite a few calls and bookings already."

"No kidding? That's great." Christian leaned in for a closer look and, as he did, his arm brushed against Molly ever so slightly.

She glanced his way and was shocked to see his expression had changed: his face was completely drained of color and he looked like he needed to sit down. Molly pushed a stool towards him and he sat slowly looking like he was in a daze.

"What's wrong? You look like you've seen a ghost, as clichéd as that sounds." She'd never seen him look like this. "Are you feeling sick?"

Christian was quiet for a moment and looked like he was gathering his thoughts. "For a minute there, I thought I did see a ghost, sort of. That name, the Olander reservation, kind of threw me. It's not a common name, and I once knew an Olander."

Molly felt the hair stand up on her arms. She knew without him saying anything that his ex-girlfriend, the one that had run out on him right before their wedding, was an Olander. She hoped it was a coincidence. A moment later, Christian confirmed her hunch.

"Heather, the girl I almost married, her last name was Olander. I haven't seen or even heard anything about her in years."

Impulsively, Molly put her hand on his arm and gave it a light squeeze. "Well, I don't know if this person is related, but it's definitely not her. The woman who booked it sounded like she was in her seventies, maybe. Her first name is Agnes, and she's coming with another woman named Helen."

"That's her aunt, and her aunt's best friend."

"Do you still think about her?" Molly asked, and immediately regretted it, thinking it was too personal and that he wouldn't want to go there. But he didn't seem to mind.

"No. I haven't in years. I'm long over it, but it was a pretty horrible time for me. It made me question everything." He looked at Molly and then explained, "It just threw me, seeing the name."

"Does she ever come back to Beauville? Have you run into her over the years?" Molly was curious, wondering if he ever really had gotten closure.

"No, I haven't seen her since then. Her family is still here, but the guy she married worked for a big four accounting firm and took a transfer to Australia shortly after their wedding. As far as I know, they are still living there."

Molly couldn't help but wonder how Christian would feel if he ever ran into his ex again? It had been a long time, but she had done some damage. Molly was glad to hear Heather was out of the country, so running into each other wasn't likely.

Christian stood up and started walking toward the door, "Let's go get your car jumped and head home."

Once he'd charged her car for a bit, the motor started easily, and Molly drove back to the ranch with Christian following her, just in case something went wrong.

"Have you eaten yet?" he asked, as they walked into the kitchen.

"Just nibbled on some cheese and crackers." Molly realized she was starting to get hungry.

"Mrs. O'Brien made a beef stew for us. She left instructions to turn it down to a low simmer, and I was doing that when you called."

"That sounds wonderful." Molly got out two bowls, as Christian sliced several pieces of crusty bread for them from the loaf Mrs. O'Brien had also baked earlier.

"A little wine to go with?" He asked as he reached for a bottle of Merlot. When Molly nodded, he opened the bottle and poured them both a glass.

They chatted easily during dinner, catching up on how their respective days had gone. The stew was delicious, just the thing for the cold winter weather, and the Merlot was smooth and easy to drink. Molly was a little surprised to find her glass was empty when they finished eating. She wasn't planning to have a second glass, but Christian refilled his and when he asked if she wanted more, it suddenly seemed like a good idea. She could feel all the tension melting out of her body and realized she had been a bit on edge, more worried than she'd realized about the inn's opening day. It was such a relief that everything had gone so smoothly.

"Feel like a game of pool?" Christian asked, after they'd cleared the table and put the dirty bowls in the dishwasher.

"Why not?" It was still early and a Friday night, so it sounded like a good idea and something different. They hadn't played yet since she'd arrived at the ranch. Christian had a finished basement that was set up like a game room, with a tournament-sized pool table, dart board, big screen TV and a small bar.

"I will warn you though, I haven't played in years, and I never was very good."

"Pool is like riding a bike, it will come back to you." Christian said, as he grabbed the bottle of wine to bring along to the basement.

Though Molly was rusty at first, it did come back to her as they got into the game. And it helped when Christian gave her a few pointers, explaining how to work angles to make the ball go where she wanted it to. At one point, he came up behind her and showed her exactly how to hold her cue lower, so she would have more control. Though Molly found it hard to concentrate when his arms were on either side of her as he demonstrated the ideal grip. She felt the energy in the room shift, and it didn't lessen when he left her side to take his own shot.

Christian, of course, won the first game easily, but Molly held her own in the second and then actually managed to win, though it was by default as Christian blew his last shot. The eight ball went into the pocket that he called, followed by the white cue ball, meaning he scratched and it was an instant loss for him. "Congrats!" he said, as Molly made a face. That wasn't the way she wanted to win.

"Hey, a win's a win." He high-fived her and, as their hands touched, Molly looked him in the eye, willing him to kiss her again.

Christian only hesitated a moment, before pulling her into his arms and bringing his lips down to hers. She felt the same sparks this time as she had when they'd first kissed, and the same disappointment when he pulled away and shook his head.

"Don't apologize again," she said quickly, as Christian opened his mouth to speak and then was quiet for a moment.

"I shouldn't have done that though. We already talked about this, how it's not a good idea." He didn't look happy as he said it.

"I think it would be a very good idea. We're obviously attracted to each other and we're married. Why not see where it goes?"

Christian looked at her in amazement. "You can't mean that. You know my track record. I don't do commitment any more. And you have to get back to Manhattan."

"We have four months to go. A lot can happen in that time. Aren't you a little curious to see how it goes?" Molly's heart was racing. She couldn't believe she was trying to talk him into having a relationship with her. It felt so brazen, but yet so right. She knew she was taking a risk and maybe he really couldn't commit to anyone, but she was hopeful that if it was meant to be they could somehow work things out.

"You'll still be going back to Manhattan." Christian insisted, as he emptied his wine glass. They'd finished the bottle between the two of them.

"Maybe I will, maybe I won't. Maybe Rose Cottage will be enough, if things go well with us. If they don't, then I will leave and you can go back to the way things were. It's really a win-win." She truly believed that Christian was capable of committing; he'd once been engaged after all.

"A win-win….okay. I think that might be the wine talking." He sighed and then said, "If you really mean this, then I'm up for it, but it's not something to decide lightly. We've both been drinking. Sleep on it, and then if you really do want to see where this could go, let me know. If you don't, just forget we ever had this conversation. And on that note, I'm going to bed." He gave her a quick hug and then took their empty glasses and the wine bottle with him, and Molly watched him walk away, enjoying the view and smiling to herself, because she knew she wasn't going to be changing her mind.

Chapter 11

Breakfast was a big hit the next morning, especially the quiche and coffee cake. The bowl of fruit that Molly had spent a good half hour preparing sat mostly untouched. Once her guests had finished eating, and had gone on their way, Molly poured herself a bowl of cereal and added a generous helping of the fruit. Someone had to eat it after all, and it was delicious. She'd cut fresh pineapple and tossed it with wild blueberries, sliced strawberries and bananas.

When she was just about done, her cell phone rang and she was excited to see that it was Meghan. They hadn't talked in over a week and Molly always looked forward to their chats. Although hearing Meghan's voice did tend to make her a little homesick for Manhattan. Meghan asked about the inn and how it was going and, once Molly had given her the update, Meghan filled her in on the real reason for her call.

"So, I ran into your boss, Ben, the other night. We'd all gone to Harry's Place on Thursday right after work." Molly loved going to Harry's Place; all the bartenders knew them, as they often met up there as it was right around the corner from the hotel and from Meghan's office.

"How is Ben?" Molly asked.

"He's great, really great, actually." That was interesting. Did she detect a hint of interest in Ben? That was something new. Molly was about to ask, when Meghan went on to say, "So, anyway, Ben was filling me in on the renovations at the hotel, and it sounds like they're actually a little ahead of schedule. He asked about you, if we'd been in touch, and if I knew when you were planning to be back in Manhattan. It sounds like he's eager for you to return as soon as you're able."

Molly's first reaction was excitement. She couldn't wait to see the improvements at The Clarendon, and it sounded like she might not have to wait as long as she'd thought for her promotion if Ben was anxious for her to return. It was everything she'd dreamed of, although she realized that she wasn't in a hurry for her time in Montana to end. Leaving here would be bittersweet.

"I can't come back before the six months are up, that's what we're agreed to. But it will be here before we know it. Time is flying."

"So you're not too miserable being there?" Meghan asked.

"No, not miserable at all. I'm enjoying it actually." Molly was about to tell Meghan about the latest development with Christian, but something held her back. Nothing had really happened yet, and she didn't want to jinx it, in case things didn't work out, after all. "Rose Cottage is keeping me busy, and I'm having fun building a business from scratch. So far so good."

"Oh, good, I'm so glad to hear it." Meghan sounded a bit distracted. Molly was just about to ask her about her love life, and if she'd imagined her interest in Ben, when Meghan said, "Shoot, I'm sorry to cut this short, but I have to run. Someone's at my door."

"Okay, I'll let you go, talk soon." Molly hung up, and started cleaning the kitchen. The rest of the day flew, as she was distracted by daydreaming about seeing Christian later. She'd woken up even more convinced that they could be really good together. Though she had to admit she had butterflies in her stomach from anticipation. Her mind was made up; she only hoped that Christian hadn't changed his.

On the way home, Molly stopped at the local market and picked up a few things for dinner, and a bottle of her favorite Cabernet. It would go well with the steaks she was planning to make. It was one of her favorite recipes: juicy rib-eyes, with a red wine reduction sauce and a delicious topping of panko crumbs mixed with blue cheese that was finished under the broiler to get the crumb topping crispy and the cheese a bit melted.

She was surprised to see Christian's truck already in the driveway when she got home. Although it was a Saturday, it was still a work day for him, and he'd mentioned briefly when she'd seen him that morning that he thought it would be a long day, as they were trying to finish up a building project that had run into some delays.

Molly parked and then brought her bags into the kitchen. She heard water running upstairs and figured that Christian was in the shower, so she decided to start getting dinner ready. She had assembled a big salad and was about to put the steaks and potatoes in the oven to bake, when Christian came down the stairs carrying a small suitcase. He looked anxious and in a hurry.

"Is everything all right?" She asked.

Christian looked at her and she saw concern and fear in his eyes. "No. I got a call to say my brother has been in a bad accident. A nurse from the hospital let me know that it's pretty serious, and he's on his way into surgery. I'm heading to the airport now. I've just booked the next flight out to Chicago. I have no idea how long I'll be gone. It depends on how he's doing. Might be a few days, might be all week. I'll call and let you know."

Molly's heart went out to him. "Do you want me to come with you?"

"No. Like I said, I have no idea how long I'll be gone, and you need to take care of Rose Cottage."

"Okay, well, at least let me drive you to the airport. You shouldn't be driving right now." Christian hesitated, but Molly insisted. "We don't need two accidents because you're distracted by worrying about your brother. Come on. The airport's not that far."

Molly turned off the oven, put on her coat, grabbed her bag and headed to the door. Christian followed, and put his suitcase in the back seat of her car.

They drove to the airport mostly in silence, after Christian had filled her in with as much as he knew about the accident. Dan had been about a mile from his apartment when a drunk driver had come around the corner and plowed into him head on. Dan lived in the city so he wouldn't have been driving that fast, but Christian didn't know the extent of his injuries and was just hoping that they weren't life-threatening.

Molly hadn't seen Dan in years. He hadn't made it for the wedding because he'd been out of the country. Christian had explained the terms of their grandfather's will, and Dan had found it amusing and had been glad that their grandfather hadn't tried to set him up, too. Christian had explained previously to Molly that their grandfather had included Dan in his will, and had left him a small share of the ranch.

Dan had gone to college in Chicago and stayed there after graduating. He'd worked at one of the big papers for several years, and then a blog he wrote on investing had taken off and now he worked for himself, investing in the stock market, sharing his successes and failures on his blog and taking the occasional freelance writing assignment to keep things interesting. At age thirty two, he was a few years younger than Christian and was also a confirmed bachelor.

"Is he dating anyone? Is there anyone you should call?" Molly asked, as she pulled into the airport parking lot.

"I have no idea. I haven't met one of his girlfriends since his college days. He says he doesn't date anyone long enough to warrant an introduction."

"That sounds familiar." Molly said, trying to make light of the moment.

"We're nothing alike." Christian said seriously, as he got out of the car and then grabbed his bag from the back seat.

"Okay. Call me with an update."

"Will do. Thanks for the ride, I appreciate it."

The plane ride to Chicago was long and bumpy, followed by a jarring stop- and-go taxi cab trip to the hospital. It reflected Christian's tense mood well. He couldn't stop worrying about Dan. He and his brother were pretty tight. There was only a two year difference between them, and they'd always gotten along great for the most part. Christian had understood why Dan had needed to get away for college, to get some distance from the small town he'd grown up in. They were definitely opposites in that regard. Christian couldn't wait to return to Beauville, after graduating from the University of Montana in Missoula. He could have gone to the Bozeman campus, which would have been closer to home, but the program at Missoula was stronger.

Dan had gotten accepted into the University of Montana at Missoula as well, but had considered it his safety school. As soon as he'd received the letter of acceptance from the University of Chicago and their excellent writing program, his mind had been made up. He'd fallen in love with the hustle and bustle of Chicago, and the idea of moving home after graduating from college had never really crossed his mind.

Besides, by the time Dan had graduated from college, he'd had a job already lined up at the Chicago Tribune, one of the country's top papers. The only reason he'd been able to get in as a fresh college graduate was because he'd done a paid internship during his sophomore year, and it had gone so well that they'd occasionally given him small stringer assignments, such as covering annual meetings of the Chicago Board Options Exchange and other related business stories.

Dan had found the world of options trading fascinating, and the more he covered it, the more he'd learned. He'd started doing a little trading himself and found he had a knack for it. Just for kicks, he'd started a blog to discuss his trading experiments, and the thought process and strategy he used for each trade. The blog had built a rabid following and questions had come pouring in from readers. That's when he'd realized that he might actually be able to develop a side business with the blog. He'd turned it into a membership site, where his blog and trading information would only be available to monthly subscribers. Dan had thought he'd make a bit of extra money, but he'd vastly underestimated the potential.

Within a year, fees from the monthly membership had exceeded three times his salary at the newspaper. In addition, he was having even more success with his trading. Enough so, that he'd decided to give notice to the paper and then make himself available as a freelancer, picking and choosing the assignments that most interested him.

All of this went through Christian's mind as he sat by his brother's bedside, waiting for him to wake up. The doctor had stopped in once to check on him, and had told Christian that Dan was lucky: he'd broken his leg in three places, but it didn't appear that there was any internal damage. The doctor had also said that the surgery had gone well, but that Dan was going to have difficulty getting around for several months.

Christian also thought of Molly as he sat waiting. He wondered what she was up to, and how nice it would have been if she had come. He knew that, if she had been sitting next to him, that just her presence would have kept him calm, and helped ease his worrying about his brother. He also realized how much he'd enjoyed coming home every day to her welcoming smile and warmth.

Finally, about twenty minutes after the doctor's visit, Dan stirred and then opened his eyes. He stared blankly around the room, and then blinked when he saw Christian. He looked both confused and pleased to see him.

"Hey buddy, how are you feeling?"

"Like shit. Like I got run over by a truck." Dan attempted a smile and then said, "I think maybe I did actually run into a truck."

"That's what they say," Christian confirmed.

"Has the doctor been in? What did he say? Can I go home today?"

"Not today. They want to keep you another twenty four hours to watch for infection. You broke your leg."

"Just the leg?"

Yeah, in three places. You're going to have a tough time getting around for a few months."

"How long?" Dan directed the question at the doctor, who had just walked into the room holding his clipboard.

"For you, at least four months. You broke your tibia and fibula, multiple breaks. You'll need physical therapy after that."

"I'll be on crutches for four months?" Dan did not look at all happy about that.

"At least. Might be longer, depends how you heal." The doctor was very matter-of-fact; it was going to take some time.

"Dan, you can do your work from anywhere, right? It's mostly all online stuff?" Christian asked.

Dan nodded and Christian continued. He'd been thinking this through while Dan had slept. Dan lived in a beautiful old brownstone, on the fourth floor, and like most of those old buildings, his didn't have an elevator. His closest friends lived nearby in similar walk-ups.

"I think you should come home with me while you recuperate. There's no way you can manage four flights of stairs every day on crutches. Plus, you know we have plenty of space at the ranch. You can stay in Gramps' old room." His grandfather's room was a spacious one, on the first floor, just a few steps from the kitchen, and was an en suite with an oversized bathroom. It would be perfect.

"I guess so." Dan didn't look thrilled at the thought of spending multiple months in Beauville.

"I'll stay at your place tonight and pack a bag for you. I'll get your laptop and whatever else you want to bring; just make me a list."

"Okay. Four months in Beauville . . . that's a really long time." Dan looked exhausted at the very idea of it and, within seconds, his eyes drifted shut and Christian knew it hadn't really sunk in yet.

Chapter 12

"How's Dan settling in?" Aunt Betty asked. She and Molly's mother had stopped by just after breakfast service to visit for a bit, and her mom wanted to try out a new recipe for the inn: a breakfast casserole made with eggs, bread, cheese and bacon and apple sausage. It sounded delicious, and while it was in the oven baking, they sat around the island bar in the kitchen drinking pumpkin spice coffee.

"As well as you could expect. He's friendly enough, but would much rather be back in Chicago. His whole life is there."

"You adjusted," Aunt Betty said.

"True, but I've also always loved it here."

"At least he's able to do his work here, that's something," her mother said.

"That's true. He spends most of his time at the kitchen table, on his laptop."

"What's he like now?" Aunt Betty was curious. "I haven't seen that boy in years."

"Well, he's very tall; taller than Christian and a bit thinner."

"No muscles then?" Aunt Betty persisted.

"Just not as muscular. I think Christian is more physically active, outside more. Dan is an indoors guy, as pale as can be. He's super-nice, though."

"I bet Linda O'Brien is happy to have him home." Her mother said, and Molly smiled. It was so true. Mrs. O'Brien seemed thrilled to have both of her boys there. She buzzed around Dan like a mother hen, constantly checking on him and bringing him little treats, like her special shakes made with chocolate ice cream and bananas.

"She thinks he's too thin and is on a mission to fatten him up."

"Is it strange having someone else in the house?" Aunt Betty asked.

"Not really, he's Christian's family after all." It actually was a little strange, though, as Molly was starting to feel very much at home, and whenever she got up in the morning or returned home at night, Dan was always there, either working in the kitchen, or lounging on the sofa in the family room watching TV. He had to be up and at work early, because of the time difference, and it wasn't like he could really go anywhere yet. The doctor had said to avoid putting weight on his leg at all for the first month, to give the bones time to start knitting together.

"In a few weeks, when he's feeling up to it, I'll have you two over for dinner, if you like."

"Definitely!" Aunt Betty was always up for an evening out, and Molly knew she loved the idea of being the first to meet Dan. There was a lot of buzz about him, evidently, among the ladies who met for coffee at the Morning Muffin. Sight unseen, Dan was considered quite the eligible catch and the match-making wheels were turning.

"Too bad he's not planning to stick around," her mother said, as she got up to check on the casserole.

"There's really no reason for him to stay here. He has a life in Chicago. Kind of like me with Manhattan," Molly reminded them gently. She knew they were both hoping that she'd decide to stay in Beauville, and that she and Christian would fall madly in love and live happily ever after. Before Christian's trip to Chicago to get Dan, Molly had had to admit she thought it could actually be a real possibility. But with Dan there, Christian had withdrawn a bit, and they hadn't really had any alone time.

"But he can do his job from anywhere right? It's been years since he's spent any time here. Maybe Beauville will grow on him." Aunt Betty expected that everyone would fall in love with Beauville, if they spent enough time here.

A blinking red light caught Molly's eye. She had her laptop perched nearby and had been checking reservations when her mother and aunt had arrived, so the screen was still up. The red light was the program's signal for a reservation cancellation. It was the second one today, so she pulled the laptop closer to get a better look.

"That's really strange," she said, as she saw that the cancellation was for the same weekend as the one that had come in earlier.

"What's strange, honey?" her mother asked.

She told them about the two cancellations within an hour for the same weekend, then asked, "When is Isabella planning to open her place?" Molly hadn't heard any updates at all, but had a feeling she knew when Isabella's grand opening might be. Two cancellations in such a short time period was too much of a coincidence.

"We should check the local paper," her mother said. "She's probably got an ad in if she's planning to open soon." Molly had the newspaper delivered each morning, but hadn't looked at it in a few days. She got up and went out to the lobby, and it was in its usual spot on the coffee table. She brought it back into the kitchen and divvied up the three sections. Minutes later, Aunt Betty found something.

"Here we go. What's the date of the cancellations?" Molly told her, and she continued, "That makes perfect sense then. Isabella has a huge ad with a buy-one-get-one opening special; two nights for the price of one. I'd expect a few more cancellations, once this gets out."

"How long is the offer good for?" It wasn't a strategy Molly would have ever advised, especially for someone new to the hospitality business. She guessed that Isabella was planning to have nine or ten rooms available, and having them booked solid on opening weekend might be a bit overwhelming.

"It looks like it's just for that weekend. She wants to start out with a splash. No surprise there."

"Would it make sense to do a similar promotion?" her mother asked.

"If I did that, it would look too reactive, for one thing. But secondly, for the type of inn that we are, I don't think a buy-one-get-one promotion is the way to go. That's not the kind of branding I want. It's too much of a discount, and would make us look desperate."

"It's not like you're having trouble renting the rooms," Aunt Betty agreed. And it was true; while they weren't sold out every night, they were mostly full on the weekends and half to three quarters full during the week, which Molly was pleased with. The reviews so far had been overwhelmingly positive, and several guests had already booked return trips later in the year.

"I have thought of doing some promotion though: special packages for different events and holidays."

"What kind of packages?" Her mother checked on the casserole again, and this time took it out of the oven and set it on the counter to cool.

"I have a few ideas in mind: a special anniversary package that would include a gift certificate to Delancey's; a spa package that would include a trip to that new day spa that's opening; and a wine dinner package, where a four course dinner would be served here with accompanying wines. I thought we could take a few reservations just for the dinner too, if local people were interested."

"That all sounds wonderful," her mother said, and then added, "Maybe you should do the wine dinner first. That could generate some local buzz I think."

"I agree. I'm going to start planning something, maybe for the weekend after Isabella opens; that gives me a month."

"Why not do the same weekend? Give Isabella a run for her money." Aunt Betty was excited for a showdown.

"No, I don't want to do that. We'll let Isabella have the spotlight for that weekend. I'm happy to wait a bit."

When Molly arrived home a little after five, Dan was just clearing his stuff off the kitchen table and getting ready to relocate to the sofa in the family room. Molly smiled at the sight of a half-full chocolate shake by his laptop.

"I need to lay off these." Dan said, as he saw Molly staring at the shake. "I've gained seven or eight pounds since I've been here."

"It's probably from being less active too. I wouldn't worry much about it."

"True, I feel like a little old man right now: stiff from sitting all day." He eased himself up from the chair and onto his crutches, and did a few laps around the kitchen. "Feels good to stretch."

"Did Mrs. O'Brien leave dinner for us?" She didn't see anything on the stove, or smell anything in the oven.

"She made a bunch of stuffed shells earlier, and put them in the fridge. Said we can heat them whenever."

"Okay, I can make us a salad, and I think we have bread still."

"Do you think Christian might be up for going out for a change?" Dan surprised her. "I'm just feeling kind of stir crazy."

"Sure, if you think you're up for it." Dan hadn't left the house once since he'd arrived.

"I think it would be okay now. It will be four weeks tomorrow."

"Did I hear something about going out?" Christian walked into the kitchen, and even though he was spotted with dried mud, he still looked good to her. His days varied from managing paper and building plans to actually being out in the fields, being hands on with whatever needed doing. Today was obviously a ranch day.

"Dan is up for dinner out somewhere," Molly said.

"Great, give me fifteen minutes to shower and change, and then let's head out."

They walked into Delancey's forty five minutes later. Dan was able to move pretty quickly on his crutches, and he'd also changed while Christian was in the shower. Molly hadn't seen him in anything other than sweats and tee-shirts since he'd arrived, and was impressed by how sharp he looked. He'd put on jeans and a hunter-green button-down shirt that highlighted his green eyes and dark blonde hair, and he'd even shaved. Molly noticed more than one female guest taking a long look as they walked by. Christian looked amazing too, as always. He was also in jeans and was wearing her favorite soft blue button-down shirt. He hadn't taken the time to shave, so there was a hint of stubble that she actually found really attractive.

They were seated quickly at a great table near where the band would soon be setting up. Dan looked pleased when he saw there was going to be entertainment.

"Impressive. Didn't know you had any places like this in Beauville now."

"A lot has changed since you lived here," Christian began. "The town has grown. Is still growing."

"So, what's good here?" Dan asked, as the waitress handed them menus. He smiled at her and Molly noticed that she immediately seemed flustered.

"Everything's good, everything. Can I get you something to drink?" She took their drink orders and then scurried off.

"I know you're getting back to normal now. The ladies here don't stand a chance." Christian said with a chuckle, and Molly thought back to what he'd told her about Dan. She hadn't really seen his flirty side until now, but could see how he'd be popular with women. He had a smoother look to him, an easy charm and a killer smile that made his green eyes pop. She could see him breaking a heart or two if he decided to date while he was here because, as he reminded them regularly, he was going back to Chicago as soon as the doctor cleared him to return.

"The steak is what's really good here." Molly told him, as the waitress returned with their drinks, and Dan told her they needed a little more time to decide.

"Okay, steak it is then." As he closed his menu, Molly noticed Travis and Traci walk in. Christian saw them too and waved them over.

"Are you guys here for dinner? Join us, we just ordered drinks."

"Great, I just had a crazy day, and told Traci I'd buy her dinner if she agreed to come out."

"He didn't have to twist my arm too hard," Traci laughed.

The waitress returned just then and pulled a chair over to their table, so there was room for all of them, and both Travis and Traci sat down.

Once they all had their drinks and had put their dinner orders in, Christian proposed a toast,

"To Dan's first night out in Beauville."

"And to many more," Travis added.

They all clicked glasses, and the conversation flowed easily as they ate their salads.

Until Traci asked Molly, "Have you heard about Isabella's opening special?"

"We've already had two cancellations because of it. I don't blame them really, it's a good deal."

"What is she doing?" Christian looked at Molly in surprise. She usually kept him posted on everything.

"I just saw the ad in today's paper. She's running an opening day special, two nights for the price of one, including weekends."

"Can she do that?" Christian addressed the question to Travis.

He hesitated for a moment, then said, "As Isabella's attorney, I shouldn't be discussing this with you, but yeah, it's totally legal."

"Just because it's legal, doesn't make it right." Traci glared at her brother, who looked decidedly uncomfortable at the direction the conversation had taken.

"It's all right," Molly assured all of them. "It's inconvenient for us, but I don't blame her for doing it. It's a business decision, something any competitor would do."

"You wouldn't do it," Traci said loyally.

"No, I would if it made sense to do it. It wouldn't have been my strategy for a grand opening though."

This caught Dan's attention. "Why not? Seems like a good idea to me."

"I'm just more cautious," Molly explained. "I'm a bit of a worrier though. We had a slow opening, just two rooms rented and that was perfect for me. I wanted to make sure everything went smoothly."

"And it did." Christian said proudly, and Molly noticed that Dan glanced at him curiously.

"Slow has never been Isabella's speed," Travis said, as he reached for another roll.

"I don't suppose you got an invite to her opening party?" Traci directed the question at Molly.

"No, when is it?"

"This Thursday, the night before she officially opens. Isn't that exactly what you did?"

Molly just nodded, and then asked, "Are you going?"

"I haven't decided yet. I don't have anyone to go with. Travis will already be there. They have an appointment just before the party begins."

"I'll go with you." Dan surprised them by saying. "I'm getting really stir crazy and that will get me out of the house. And I can be the lone family representative or spy, however you want to look at it." His smile was full of mischief, and Molly thought she saw Traci blush slightly. Yes, Dan was definitely feeling better.

Chapter 13

Molly wasn't surprised when two more cancellations came in the following week. Rose Cottage had gone from fully booked for the weekend, to half-empty since Isabella's ad had run. Aunt Betty was furious and had been ranting and raving about it all week, even though Molly explained that in the overall scheme of things it really wasn't a big deal. Any competitor might do the same thing, and it wasn't personal, it was just business.

Once Thursday arrived, Molly was actually looking forward to Isabella's opening night party. Not because she was planning to attend; neither she nor Christian had been invited. But, because Dan was going to the party with Traci, it would be her first night alone with Christian in over a month. At breakfast, he'd casually asked if she wanted to grab a bite to eat somewhere in Bozeman for a change, and she was looking forward to it.

As soon as her guests finished their wine and cheese and left for dinner, Molly put everything away and then headed home. When she walked in the door, she heard the shower running and knew it was Dan getting ready to go out with Traci. She would be picking him up as he still wasn't cleared to drive. Christian wasn't home yet, and Molly didn't expect him for at least another hour. He'd called earlier, and said one of his projects was behind schedule and they'd be working a little late every day this week to catch up.

Molly decided to draw a bath and soak for a while. She was usually more of a shower girl, preferring to get in and get out and on her way. But every now and again, there was nothing like a luxurious, relaxing soak. A few days after she'd arrived, and had shown her around the ranch, her mother surprised her with a small bottle of tangerine-scented bubble bath.

"When I saw that in the store, I had to get it for you. You might as well enjoy that hot tub while you can."

It really was an amazing soaking tub. You had to step up to it. The two steps led to a beautiful marble platform and a shiny white porcelain oversized tub, with jets at either end. Molly set a few small candles around the tub. As the water was filling it, she lit the candles and found a magazine she hadn't looked at yet. She added the bubble bath when the tub was halfway full and then, once it was ready, she stepped in to a sea of sweet smelling bubbles. The citrusy scent of the bubble bath mixed deliciously with the vanilla buttercream aroma of the candles. She sunk into the warmth of the water, leaned her head back against the tub edge and closed her eyes.

She stayed like that until she heard the door downstairs open and the familiar tread of Christian's footsteps coming down the hall. As soon as she heard the sound of his shower, she decided it was time to leave the cocoon of warmth and start getting ready. She toweled off, put on moisturizer, combed out her hair and then stared at her open closet for several minutes, before deciding on her favorite bootleg jeans and a rose pink vee-neck sweater. The soft cashmere was both warm and flattering.

Fifteen minutes later, her hair was blown dry, and her mascara, blush and lipstick applied, and her boots were on. She'd chosen the pair of cowboy boots that she'd fallen in love with during her first week in Beauville.

When she came downstairs Christian was sitting at the kitchen island bar, reading the local paper. He looked up when he saw her.

"You look great! Are you ready to go?"

"Thanks, I'm ready." He looked amazing too, and there was a sudden charge in the air that she hadn't felt in weeks, since Dan arrived. She could tell by the look in Christian's eyes that he was feeling it too. He was wearing jeans as well and the shirt that Molly had mentioned before to him that she loved, the navy-blue button-down. It looked great on him. It made his hair look darker and his eyes a deeper blue.

They chatted easily during the drive to Bozeman and listened to a Pearl Jam CD. Christian was a huge fan of the band and had seen them live a few times, and the CD was from the last show he went to. The ride flew by and, before she knew it, they arrived at a tiny Italian restaurant that was tucked away on a side street in a not so fashionable area, but it was completely packed. Christian had called ahead to make a reservation so they didn't have to wait, and they were seated immediately at a small table by a window.

Their waitress came right over and Christian ordered a bottle of red wine, an Italian Merlot. While they were looking over the menu, Molly thought she overheard several people at a table nearby speaking Italian. She glanced at Christian in surprise and he explained, "This place is out of the way, but has a great reputation for being really authentic. Almost every time I've come here I've heard someone speaking Italian."

"That sounds like a good sign."

"It is. I stumbled onto this restaurant years ago, and have been coming back ever since."

Molly saw a plate of cheese ravioli and meatballs go by, and decided to order that once the waitress told her the pasta was homemade and a specialty of the house. Christian ordered the chicken parmesan. The waitress warned them that there might be a little bit of a wait, as the kitchen was backed up. She brought out a basket of hot, crusty bread and salads with their house Italian dressing, and they dug in.

After the waitress removed their salad plates, they did have a bit of a wait before their dinners came out. It was nice to relax and not feel rushed, and Molly was happy to just enjoy Christian's company as they sipped their wine, which was phenomenal: rich and silky.

"I'm so glad we did this," she said impulsively.

"You are? Good, I'm glad." Christian took a sip of wine and then continued, "I hope it hasn't been too difficult for you, having Dan stay with us."

"Of course not, he's your brother," Molly assured him. "It's actually been nice getting to know him."

"The timing just isn't ideal. Not that there's ever a good time for these things, but you know what I mean."

Molly just nodded and took another sip of wine. Christian was quiet for a long moment, and looked like he was debating whether or not to say something.

Finally, he set down his wine glass and said, "We never did finish our discussion, what we were talking about the night before I left to get Dan. Though there's probably nothing to really discuss any more. Dan's arrival ended that possibility." He sounded regretful but fairly certain.

"I never changed my mind." Molly put her hand on his and smiled, and he set his wine glass down, totally taken by surprise.

"Really? You're sure?"

She nodded and he was speechless for a moment. The waitress arrived just then with their dinners and set them down.

"Even with Dan there?" Christian persisted. He was clearly surprised that she was still interested.

"We can be discreet, and besides he's an adult, he'll deal with it." Molly thought to herself that she didn't think it was likely to surprise Dan. She'd noticed him looking at both of them questioningly over the past few weeks; undoubtedly he'd picked up a vibe or two.

"Okay, well, let's eat and then get out of here." Christian grinned, and Molly smiled back and took a bite of her pasta. It was out of this world, light and flavorful, but Molly's mind was elsewhere. She was thinking ahead to what would happen when they arrived back at the ranch, and the butterflies in her stomach danced in nervous anticipation.

They declined dessert and packed more than half of their dinners in to-go boxes. The ride home was mostly quiet, except for the sound of the Pearl Jam CD playing again. Molly was full and happy from the good food and wine, and eager to get home. When they pulled into the driveway, the lights inside were still off, so Molly realized that Dan must still be out with Traci.

They put their takeout boxes in the refrigerator, and then Christian asked if she wanted a little wine.

"Just a half glass please." He poured them both small glasses of wine, and then brought them into the family room and set them down on the coffee table.

"Should we put a movie on?" he asked as he took a step closer to her.

"If you want to," she agreed, and then leaned in as he wrapped his arms around her.

"I'd rather do this." He kissed her then and Molly sank into him, running her hands along the back of his neck and lightly through his hair, as he teased her lips and then kissed his way along her throat and then back to her lips.

They stayed like that for a while, lost in each other, until Molly faintly heard the sound of a car door and then low voices laughing. Christian heard the same and then pulled back.

"Let's go upstairs." He shut off the light in the family room, so Dan would just assume they'd both gone up to bed, and then picked up their wine glasses and looked back at Molly. She smiled and followed him up the stairs.

Molly woke earlier than usual the next morning. She felt deliciously relaxed and lazy as she stretched her arms, rolled onto her side and remembered that she was in Christian's bed. He was already awake too, and leaned over and kissed her lightly on the forehead.

"Morning. Sleep well?"

"Never better," she said, and stretched again, feeling happy.

"I'm not ready to get up just yet, are you?" He ran his fingers lightly down Molly's arm and she shivered.

"I'm pretty comfortable right here." She smiled and snuggled closer to him, and he pulled her in even tighter and brought his lips down to hers.

They finally dragged themselves out of bed, and Molly was in a happy glow all day, replaying the events of the previous night over and over again in her mind. She couldn't stop thinking about Christian. Their lovemaking was even better than she could have imagined. They just felt so right together. At least that was how she felt, and it seemed as though Christian felt the same. She'd been a little worried that things might be awkward, or that Dan would know instantly the minute he saw them together. But it was wonderfully normal when they met up in the kitchen for breakfast.

Christian, as usual, had left earlier to do his rounds on the ranch and then had come back to eat a little before seven. Dan was already up and on his laptop by then, and Molly was having her coffee at the island countertop. They all ate breakfast together, same as ever, and then went on their separate ways. Dan didn't give either one of them a second glance, much to Molly's relief. It's not that she would have minded him knowing that they'd entered a different stage in their relationship, she just didn't want to be in his face about it.

Her day at the inn went smoothly as they were only at half-capacity, so it was easy to manage. She was looking forward to an evening in with Christian and Dan. They still had the stuffed shells Mrs. O'Brien had made the day before that they could heat up, and Christian mentioned that there was a movie that looked good that they could watch.

They were halfway through the movie when Molly's cell phone rang, and she saw it was the answering service for the inn. It was the first time she'd gotten an evening after-hours call and wondered what the emergency was. She hoped it was something minor, as she'd told all the guests to call if they needed anything, but so far no one had.

"Hello?"

"Is this Molly?" She confirmed that it was, and the answering service rep continued, "You have an emergency message from Isabella Graham. She is asking you to please call as soon as possible. She'd like to send several guests over immediately."

Molly thanked her, and then called the number she'd been given.

"Hello?" The voice that answered sounded anxious, not like Isabella at all.

"Isabella? It's Molly."

"Molly? Oh, thank God you called back so soon. Thank you. I'm in a bit of a jam here. There's no hot water on the second floor right now and I can't get anyone here until tomorrow morning to fix whatever is wrong. I have three rooms of guests I'd like to send your way, on me, if you have the room?" Molly was shocked into silence for a long moment, which seemed to make Isabella nervous. "I already tried The Sleepy Willow motel and they're totally booked up. Please tell me you have room?"

"I do, of course I do. Send them right over. I'll leave now to meet them."

Molly hung up the phone and jumped up to head to the inn. Christian had already figured out what was going on from what he'd heard, and Molly filled him in on the rest.

Less than ten minutes later Molly was back at the inn and picked out the three rooms for her incoming guests. She put out a plate of cookies and some lemonade, in case they felt like a little nibble or cold drink when they arrived. Interestingly, two of the parties were the ones that had cancelled their reservations with the inn earlier in the week to go to Isabella's. They were full of apologies when they arrived, and less than complimentary about their experience at Isabella's.

"She's just as nice as can be, putting us up here, but it really is a disaster over there. No hot water, can you imagine?" Mrs. Cleeson and her sister, Mrs. Rice, were not impressed.

"Her cookies aren't as good as yours either, dear," Mrs. Rice said, as she grabbed two more for good measure, before they headed off to their rooms.

A half hour later, all the new guests were settled into their rooms and Molly was on her way back to the ranch.

***

The house was quiet when Molly returned home. The news was playing on the TV, but there was no sign of Christian or Dan. Dan's bedroom door was shut and the light off, so Molly guessed that he'd likely gone to bed earlier. She saw a light on in Christian's den and headed down the hall towards the open door. Christian was sitting at his desk, flipping through an old photo album. There was a small fire going, and as usual Toby was curled up at his feet.

Christian looked up and smiled, when he saw Molly standing in the doorway. "Everything work out okay?"

"Yes, everyone is settled in for the night. Poor Isabella, that's an awful thing to have happen on any night, let alone her first night." Molly really did sympathize.

"Worked out well that you had the rooms available."

"I suppose it did." Molly smiled. "What are you up to?"

"Just going through some old boxes of my grandfather's stuff. Come see."

Molly walked over to the desk and glanced at the open book of pictures. Though the pictures were mostly black and white and somewhat faded, she still recognized many of them as being of Christian's grandfather and grandmother, and a few were of

Christian and Dan when they were younger, along with their parents.

"Is it hard for you to look at these?" she asked softly.

"It's not as hard as I thought it would be," he admitted. "I couldn't do it until now though."

Molly understood that. When her father died, neither she nor her mother had been ready to look through photos until months after the funeral.

"After you left, Dan went right to bed, said he wasn't feeling great. I didn't want to keep watching the movie without you, and actually came looking for something of my grandmother's that I thought you might like." Christian had a shy smile on his face, as he dipped into the old cardboard box and pulled out a thick cookbook that was bulging at the seams and was faded with both age and extensive use. He handed it to her and waited for her reaction.

Molly pulled up a chair and started flipping through the pages, many of which were dog-eared and stained with use. Little scraps of paper were stuffed into the pages as well, recipes that his grandmother had noted down, or clipped out of newspapers, with handwritten notes such as 'Make again', or 'Try real soon'.

"My grandfather told me once that he gave that cookbook to her when they were first married, and she always treasured it and just kept adding to it. I think he'd want you to have it."

"Really? Thank you so much, I'm honored." Molly felt her eyes water, as she turned the pages.

"She loved to cook, just like you do," Christian said.

"Do you remember any of her favorite recipes?"

He thought for a moment, and then said, "Everything she made was good. I used to really love her stuffed steak with mushroom gravy. She always made that for my grandfather's birthday. She made the best blueberry muffins, too."

"I can't wait to read through this. I'm sure I'll get some great ideas to try out at the inn."

Christian stood up and stretched. "Do you want to finish watching the movie?" He asked, and then added in a mischievous tone, "Or we could just head to bed."

"I'm not really that tired yet," Molly said, still distracted by the book.

Christian wrapped his arms around her from behind, and then whispered in her ear, "I'm not at all tired either."

Molly laughed at that. "Oh, okay. Let's head upstairs then. I can come back to this in the morning."

Chapter 14

The rest of the weekend went wonderfully, and the following month too. Molly and Christian had already settled into a routine of sorts, and now the only real difference was when they went upstairs to go to bed, they no longer went to separate bedrooms. Molly suspected that Dan had an idea of what was going on, but if he did, he never said anything.

Molly however was aware that the clock was ticking. Somehow four months had already gone by, and the six month deadline was coming up quickly. She loved being with Christian and running the inn, but her dream job was just within reach. Maybe there was a way for her and Christian to have a long distance relationship for a while. Then again, would Christian even want their relationship to continue? Things seemed to be going well enough, but neither of them had mentioned what would actually happen when they reached the six month mark, and Molly knew he had commitment issues.

All of this went through her mind as she drove to the inn to meet with Janie Summers, the caterer Isabella had used for her barbeque. Molly had spoken with Janie by phone, and she'd thought Molly's idea for a wine dinner at the inn was an excellent one and was happy to handle the cooking and serving. They were meeting today to go over the menu and wine pairings. Though Molly was flattered that Travis and Traci suggested she do the cooking herself, and admitted intrigued by the idea, she also wanted to make sure that her first wine dinner was a success, and that everything went smoothly. She thought the best way to do that was to leave the cooking and serving to the professionals, and to just oversee everything.

She did have some definite ideas for what dishes she'd like to serve, and when Janie arrived and they planned out the dinner, all the items they chose were favorites and mostly things she had made before. So, her plan was to pay close attention to how Janie set everything up, how much food she bought, what she did ahead versus what she cooked on site, so that when and if she wanted to try herself, she'd have a game plan to go by.

Shortly after Janie left, Molly's mother and aunt stopped by to say hello. It was a little before 3 and Molly had some down time before cocktail hour began. Her mother and aunt loved helping out at the inn, but Molly didn't want to burn them out either, so they had settled on a schedule of just having them each work a shift one day a week, which gave Molly a little break. They also took turns baking dishes to be used for breakfast as well, though Molly did most of the actual daily cooking.

"So, we have a little bone to pick with you," Aunt Betty said, as soon as they were settled around the island bar in the kitchen.

"Oh?" Molly simply asked. She had no idea what she might have done, and her aunt didn't seem the least bit angry. Just dramatic, as usual.

"You were seen kissing Christian! We're so happy for you." It must have been when they'd gone to the movies last weekend. Christian had kissed her briefly before they'd got into his truck. Both Betty and her mother leaned in eagerly, and looked thrilled at this piece of gossip. Molly hadn't said anything earlier, because she didn't want to get their hopes up.

"We're enjoying each other's company," she admitted. "But it's still so new. That's why I didn't say anything sooner."

"Well, honey, at least it's a step in the right direction," her aunt said, and her mother smiled in approval.

"We heard some interesting gossip about Isabella too," Betty said. "Mary-Ellen from the Ladies League overheard her telling someone at the Morning Muffin that she doesn't know how you can stand running the inn. She said there's nothing fun in it. Sounds like she's had enough and might want to sell."

"No kidding? That didn't take long." Molly wasn't surprised though. She knew that the turnover for bed and breakfasts was unusually high. So many people went into it thinking it would be easy and fun, and sometimes it could be. But there were also plenty of other times when it was anything but fun or glamorous. Molly loved it though, and compared to running The Clarendon, it was a piece of cake.

"Maybe you should buy it," Aunt Betty suggested. "Since you're going to be staying. That would make so much sense, and it's just down the road; you could easily oversee both places.

Molly had to admit, the idea was tempting, but premature. "I'm not sure if I'm going to be staying here," she reminded them. "If I do, then it's certainly something to consider."

"Dan, do you have any plans tonight?" Molly asked. They were in the kitchen having breakfast, and it was the day of the wine dinner.

"Yeah, my social calendar is so full, you know that." He grinned and then added, "I'm all yours, what did you have in mind?"

"Travis can't make it tonight to the wine dinner, he has a client coming in from out of town. I thought if you were up to it, that you might want to go with Christian. Traci will be there too. She and Travis were going together."

"Is this a setup?" he asked, and looked intrigued at the idea. He and Traci had had a great time at Isabella's opening party.

"No, not at all. I just thought it might be fun for you to get out."

"Oh, okay. Sure then, thanks for thinking of me. It will be nice to get out and about. Even better next week when this cast finally comes off." Dan had stopped using crutches a few weeks ago and was getting around pretty well without them.

"Great, I'll see you all tonight then." Molly rinsed her coffee cup out and put it in the dishwasher. She grabbed her purse, and was about to head out the door when her cell phone rang and the number that came up on the caller ID made her set her bag back down again. It was Ben calling from The Clarendon. She took a deep breath and answered the call.

"Hello."

"Molly? It's Ben, how are you?"

"Great, how's everything going?" Molly sat back down at the island bar.

"Spectacular! And I have even better news. Molly, everything is ahead of schedule. The GM spot is yours now, as soon as you can get here. When's the earliest you can be here?"

Molly's head was spinning. It was really happening, the promotion to GM could be hers if she wanted it! "I'd have to get back to you, but about a month I think."

"Okay, we can work with that. Call me to confirm in the next few days, and congrats! You deserve this."

"Thank you," Molly said softly, and hung up the phone in a daze.

"Everything okay?" Dan asked, and Molly jumped. She'd totally forgotten that he was there. She wondered how much of the conversation he'd overheard, and tried to recall what she'd actually said.

"You know, I think you're really good for my brother." Dan said with a serious look on his face. "I've never seen him this relaxed and happy." Then he added, "Don't mean to keep you, I know you need to run."

Molly didn't even know how to respond, so she just grabbed her bag and ran.

***

"So, I sort of overheard something this morning," Dan began, as he and Christian headed off to Rose Cottage for the wine dinner. "I debated whether or not to say anything because it's really none of my business, but then I figured if it was me, I'd want to know."

"What are you talking about?" Christian asked, as he focused on avoiding a pot hole as they drove onto the main road.

"I think Molly got a job offer this morning. I overheard her on the phone and she seemed so excited for a minute, like she won the lottery or something. Said something about earliest she could get there was in a month, and she'd have to get back to them in a few days."

Christian said nothing in response.

"Listen, I'm not stupid, I can see that you're crazy about her. I just thought you should know, that you guys should talk, figure it out. It'd be nice if she stayed."

"Yeah, that would be nice." Christian agreed in a clipped tone.

"Just talk to her."

Chapter 15

Molly was in a panic. Her guests were due to arrive in about ten minutes and Janie Summers, the caterer, was lying flat on her back. Everything had gone so well up until this point. She'd done a great job marketing the wine dinner, and there was a ton of interest. All thirty tickets had quickly sold out and there was already a waiting list for the next dinner. They'd picked out a fabulous menu and exquisite wines to match. Everything was going so smoothly, until Janie passed out cold in the kitchen.

Molly pressed a cool cloth against her forehead and within seconds her eyes fluttered open.

"Janie, are you okay? Can you sit up?"

"I think so." She sat up slowly.

"What happened? Do you want us to call 911?"

"No! No need for that. I'm just a little lightheaded. I feel like I'm fighting something off and really haven't eaten much of anything all day; I've no appetite."

Molly felt her forehead again, the area that the cold cloth hadn't touched, and was immediately concerned.

"Janie, you're burning up!"

Aunt Betty and Molly's mother were hovering nearby, and Aunt Betty piped up, "Two of the regulars at the Morning Muffin have been out with the flu, it's going around."

"We need to get you home," Molly said.

"I can't leave you stranded," Janie protested weakly.

"Mom, can you and Aunt Betty give Janie a ride home?"

"We'll be right back to help you," her mother said, as she and Aunt Betty helped Janie out.

Molly looked around the kitchen, panicking inside, and trying hard not to show it. Janie's assistants, the three young girls who would be serving drinks and dinner tonight, stood wide-eyed, waiting for direction.

Molly took a deep breath. She could do this. Janie had gone through the schedule with her and much of the work was already done. The appetizers had been made ahead of time and just needed to be reheated, the side dishes of mashed potatoes and caramelized Brussels sprouts were already baking in the oven and the salads were plated and lined up on the kitchen counter ready to be delivered. But, Molly still had to cook the first course, which was sautéed scallops over risotto, and the main course which was a lazy lobster casserole. She had actually asked Janie to make that dish and had given her the recipe to follow. It was one of Molly's favorites, something she'd made a million times and should be able to do in her sleep.

She started on the risotto first, as that would take about a half hour, and then the scallops would be just a few minutes in a hot pan. The risotto itself was simple, just time consuming as you had to keep an eye on it and stir the broth in a little bit at a time, so that the end result would be rich and creamy. Once she got the risotto started, she then turned to the lobster casserole. It was relatively simple. All the dish required was fresh lobster, crushed Ritz crackers, butter, chopped fresh parsley and a drizzle of sherry to finish. Before she fainted, Janie had just taken several large bags of freshly shucked lobster meat out of the refrigerator. They sat waiting on the counter top. Molly got busy filling several large trays full of the lobster, then mixed in the crumbs, butter and parsley. A drizzle of sherry, and they were ready to go into the oven when she pulled the side dishes out.

By the time her mother and aunt returned, the risotto was finished, and the girls had served several rounds of drinks and passed hot appetizers. When they brought out the salads, Molly started searing the scallops. The key was to make sure they were completely dry before putting them in the hot pan with a bit of olive oil and butter. Dry scallops ensured a nicely browned crust. Once all the scallops were cooked, she added a bit of minced shallot, white wine and a generous amount of butter. She let it all cook down quickly into a velvety sauce, then stirred in a little fresh thyme and a pinch of salt and pepper. Then she began plating them, by spooning a circle of sauce on the dish, then set two scallops in the middle and added a garnish of slivered parsley on top.

When her mother and Aunt Betty returned to the kitchen, Molly told them she had things under control and they should go enjoy their dinners too. The girls did a great job serving and cleared the plates and once the main course was served without incident, Molly started to relax. The only thing left was dessert, which was Janie's special cheesecake topped with a decadent cherry bourbon sauce. The cheesecake was chilling in the refrigerator and the sauce was on a low simmer. Molly was just about done plating the cheesecakes when Christian walked into the kitchen.

"Hi." She was surprised to see him. "Is everything going okay out there?"

Christian looked around the kitchen, there was no one there but Molly.

"I just came to say hello, and see how you are doing. Where's Janie?"

"Mom and Aunt Betty took her home right before everyone got here. She came down with something."

Christian still looked confused. "But who did everything then?"

"Well, Janie did most of the work before she left. I just finished up."

"She did all the cooking before we got here?"

"That was me, the scallops and lobster dishes," she admitted, and couldn't help asking, "were they okay?"

"Are you kidding? They were amazing. I knew you could cook, but that was really something." Christian looked so impressed and Molly felt a thrill of accomplishment. As stressed out as she'd been with Janie gone, she was now on a bit of a high that it was over and had gone well, and she'd really enjoyed doing it.

Molly knew she needed to talk to Christian, though, as soon as possible, to see if they were on the same page, and if he wanted their relationship to continue once they hit the six month mark. She'd thought about little else all day and had realized that a long-distance relationship would never work. Manhattan was too far away and the GM job too all-consuming. She'd thought about a lot of different scenarios, but the only one that really made her feel a sense of peace and happiness was being here, in Montana with Christian. Although the GM job had once been her dream, the thought of being in Manhattan, alone, just didn't hold the appeal that it once had. She hoped that Christian wanted her to stay. In her heart, she felt that he did, but she worried that she might be fooling herself. After all, Isabella had once thought that she and Christian were on the same page too.

***

"I think you should go back to Manhattan," Christian said. He and Molly were in the den. Molly was sipping a small glass of Pinot Noir, and had just gotten home from Rose Cottage and was starting to unwind. Christian was staring into a rocks glass filled with nothing but scotch.

Molly had very tentatively asked Christian where he thought things were going with them, as they were only a month away from the all- important six month deadline. She hadn't said a thing about Ben's phone call or the promotion, because she'd decided to stay in Montana instead, if Christian would have her.

"But what if I want to stay instead?" Her voice shook a little as she asked the question, and she was suddenly feeling unsure of Christian's feelings. Could she have misread him so completely?

"Dan told me about your phone call this morning. Sounds like congratulations are in order." His tone was dull and flat as he continued to sip his drink. Molly's heart sank; she should have told him earlier.

"Yes, I got the promotion. But maybe I want to stay here instead? Do you want me to stay?" Because that was what she really needed to know. How did Christian feel about her?

"I think you should go back to Manhattan," he repeated.

"You don't want me to stay, even if I want to?" Molly felt hot tears spring up and turned away to collect herself.

Christian set his glass down and then wrapped his arms around her in what felt like a good-bye hug.

"I don't have a very good track record," he began. "I've loved being with you." His voice broke a little as he continued, "But I can't guarantee anything long-term. I can't have you give up your dream job for me. What if it doesn't work out?"

"We could try having a long-distance relationship?" Molly pleaded.

"That could never work," he said simply and let her go.

"No, I suppose not," she said softly, and then walked out of the den, dumped the rest of her wine in the kitchen sink, and went to bed, alone.

The next month was brutal. Christian kept his distance and worked late almost every night, and when he got home, he went straight into his den and shut the door, so they hardly saw each other. Molly tried to focus on Rose Cottage, and added another wine dinner after the one that was already scheduled. She needed the extra work to keep her busy and help pass the time, which seemed to be crawling along at a painfully slow pace. She'd waited a day before calling Ben to formally accept the GM role, just in case Christian came to his senses and changed his mind, but that didn't happen.

***

Molly was on her second cup of coffee and kept an eye on the clock; she needed to head to the inn to start breakfast service soon. She was about to take her last sip when Mrs. O'Brien walked in the door, a bit earlier than usual.

"Good morning," Molly said half-heartedly.

Mrs. O'Brien set her bag down, and then poured herself a coffee and joined Molly at the island bar.

"I was hoping to catch you before you headed out the door."

"Is everything all right?"

"Everything is fine with me. But I'm worried about you and Christian. The two of you have been moping around for weeks."

"I'm heading back to Manhattan soon."

"You took that job, the promotion at the hotel?"

Molly nodded. She barely had the energy to talk these days.

"What does Christian say about this?"

"It was his idea, once he heard about the offer. I told him I wanted to stay, but he told me to go." Mrs. O'Brien pursed her lips and frowned at that, then took a long sip of coffee.

"He told me the truth about your arrangement, you know. The day after you and I met. It's a good thing you did for all of us."

Molly just smiled miserably, fighting back the tears once again.

"It's more than that, though, isn't it? The two of you fell in love, anyone can see that."

Molly sighed. "I thought so, but it seems like I was wrong."

"He'll come to his senses. Just give him some time."

"I'm running out of time. I fly back in a week."

"He'll come around." Mrs. O'Brien seemed sure of it, but Molly had her doubts.

The next week was a whirlwind, as Molly had hired a woman that Traci had recommended to manage the inn while she was in Manhattan, and spent her last week in Beauville training her on how they did things. Ann Rivers had worked at a motel in Bozeman for several years before having children. After being a full-time mom for almost ten years, she was ready to return to the work-force. Molly's mother and aunt had volunteered to handle everything, but Molly didn't want to put that much on their shoulders. Instead, she asked them to continue working a shift each and to mentor Ann, and continue baking as much as they'd like.

The night before she was due to fly back to Manhattan, she went to her mother's house for dinner.

"I really don't see why the two of you couldn't work this out. Plenty of people do the long-distance thing these days," Aunt Betty said, as she opened a second bottle of Merlot and topped off their glasses. They were sitting around the kitchen table, full from her mother's lasagna and had been chatting away for several hours.

Molly sighed and took another sip of wine. They'd had this conversation or some variation of it several times over the past few weeks. "I actually agree with you. Christian doesn't though. He says he doesn't want to hold me back from my dream job."

"As much as I'd like to see you stay, honey, I understand Christian's feelings on this too," her mother said. "If he really loves you, he wouldn't want to stand in your way. This is the job you've been working towards for years."

"But, I told him I wouldn't take it, that I wanted to stay." Molly felt completely empty inside.

"Sure you did, and I know you would have. But you'd also be giving up your dream. That's a lot to ask of someone, and a big weight on his shoulders if for some reason things didn't work out. He might be afraid you'd always wonder what could have been."

"So, what do I do?" Molly felt the tears welling up again. She should be thrilled to be starting her new job, but instead she was stressed out and utterly miserable. Her mother reached over, took her hand and squeezed it gently.

"You go back to Manhattan and you start that great new job, and you enjoy every minute of it. I firmly believe, and always have, that things happen for a reason and if something is meant to be, it will be. Maybe your Mr. Right is in Manhattan and you just haven't met him yet. You never know."

"You're right." Molly admitted, though the very last thing she was interested in was meeting someone new. She forced herself to smile and to look on the bright side. "Maybe the two of you will have to come to Manhattan soon for a visit; you're both long over-due."

"Absolutely!" Aunt Betty agreed with enthusiasm. "We'll have a girls' weekend. We'll start thinking about when to come and what to do. We'll have to see a show of course, and go visit the usual suspects in Brooklyn, and shop. It will be fun to play tourist with you."

"Call us as soon as your plane lands, honey." Her mother always insisted that Molly call to let her know she arrived safely whenever she traveled.

"Of course. I'm really going miss you both." Molly admitted. It had been wonderful spending so much time with her family. She was really going to miss that.

"Oh, honey, you'll be too busy to miss us! And we'll be there to bother you before you know it." Aunt Betty gave her a big hug, and then Molly hugged her mother as well and said her goodbyes. Her flight was at 6 am the next morning, and she wanted to be at the airport for 5.

Christian drove her to the airport the next day. It was still dark out as they drove, and neither one of them spoke much. There wasn't anything left to say. The sun was just starting to come up as they pulled into the airport parking lot. Christian grabbed her bags and walked her over to the curbside check-in. Molly checked her bags and then went to say good-bye to Christian. He stood waiting and, as Molly walked toward him, he held his arms open and pulled her in for a hug.

"Have a safe flight. Good luck with the new job!" He smiled and tried to look cheerful, but failed miserably. Molly could see the sadness in his eyes.

"I'm really going to miss you," she said and her voice broke.

Christian pulled her closer and touched his lips to hers for a moment. Molly sank into the kiss and he hesitated, and then kissed her back with everything that he had. Finally, he pulled back and simply said, "I'd better let you go catch your plane."

Chapter 16

"My dear Molly, we are just so thrilled that you're back." Mrs. Foyle and her little dog Daisy were on their way to tea when Molly ran into them in The Clarendon's lobby.

"Thank you! I'm very happy to be here."

"Oh, and dear, congratulations. Your promotion is very well deserved."

Molly thanked Mrs. Foyle again, and watched as the old lady swept out to her waiting town car. The Clarendon had several of these vehicles available for their guests on a first-come, first-served basis, and Mrs. Foyle had a standing reservation nearly every afternoon.

Molly was settling in nicely to the new role. Ben had stayed for several weeks to help transition her into her new responsibilities before he moved on to his new position heading up one of their newer properties. He was based just a few miles away and easily available by phone if she had any questions. So far, she hadn't though. The new role wasn't all that different from what she'd been doing as assistant GM; she just had more decision making and trouble-shooting to do, which suited her well.

One nice thing about the role was that it kept her very busy. She was putting in extra time as well, at least in the first few weeks, to get up to speed and to have something else to focus on. By the time she got home from work on most evenings, she was too tired to do much more than fall into bed. She'd only talked to Christian once since she'd been back. He'd called at exactly the one month mark, to say hello and see how things were going. She'd simply told him everything was great, that the job was going well. She left out the fact that she'd cried herself to sleep for the first week. Their conversation had been brief and both had promised to keep in touch, but it was going on three months now and she hadn't heard from Christian again, nor had she called him. She was looking forward to this weekend though, as her mother and aunt were arriving on Saturday and staying until Tuesday. Molly had arranged to take Sunday and Monday night off, so they could spend some time together.

A little before six, Molly wrapped up for the day and headed off to Harry's bar to meet Meghan for their usual Thursday night drink.

Meghan was already sitting at the bar sipping a glass of wine when Molly arrived and settled into the seat next to her. Jimmy, their favorite bartender, was over in a flash to take her order and moments later returned with a glass of Cabernet.

"So, how was your week?" Meghan asked.

"Crazy, as usual." Molly laughed and took a sip of her wine. It was delicious and, after a few more sips, she felt herself start to relax. It had been a long week, with long hours and although she loved it and was grateful for the opportunity, she was also a bit surprised to find that she didn't feel the same sense of excitement she'd always felt before. It was like something was missing.

"Well, you were pretty much doing the job before, even without the title." Meghan said, when Molly tried to explain how she was feeling. "Maybe it's just a bit of a letdown now that you're finally in the role and it's not as different as you'd imagined."

"Maybe. I suppose that could be it," Molly agreed.

"Or maybe your priorities are just different now." Molly knew Meghan was referring to Christian.

"That's very much over," she said softly.

"You're sure?" When Molly nodded, Meghan continued, "Okay, well, if you're sure, there's someone I'd like you to meet. He's a friend of Ben's, actually. Ben wants to have us all over to his place for dinner after work tomorrow." Meghan and Ben had been dating now for several months and Molly was happy for them both.

"I don't know." Molly hesitated. The idea of a date with someone else held little appeal.

"It's not really a date. Think of it as dinner with friends. It'll be super- casual. If there's a connection, great; if not, no worries."

Most people would definitely have considered Kyle Thompson a catch. He was tall, dark, handsome and most of all, nice. He was a college friend of Ben's and had recently relocated to Manhattan. Molly enjoyed talking to him. He had a great sense of humor and was passionate about his work as an architect. There was absolutely nothing wrong with him, except that he wasn't Christian. At the end of the evening, when he asked her to have dinner with him sometime, she agreed because she liked his company and because she didn't have a good enough reason to say no. Christian wasn't in the picture any longer, and Kyle really did seem like a great guy.

When her mother and Aunt arrived late Saturday afternoon, they hopped a cab to Molly's apartment and she met them there as soon as she was done with work. The small apartment was full of life with the two of them in it, and they had stopped along the way to pick up some snacks, cheese and crackers and a bottle of wine, which Aunt Betty opened as soon as Molly walked in the door. They had tickets to see Mamma Mia the next night, and reservations at Becco for dinner before the show, so on their first night in town, they just wanted to relax and catch up and, maybe, if they felt like it, have a pizza delivered.

Her mother and aunt were of course thrilled to hear about Molly's upcoming date. "It's good to get out there and meet new people," Aunt Betty said, when Molly expressed hesitation that she was ready to really start dating again.

"It's okay if he just turns out to be a friend," her mother said. "You can always use a good friend, and maybe it will turn into more. Just take it one day at a time," she advised.

"Have you seen Christian around? How is he?" Molly couldn't help but ask.

Her mother and aunt exchanged looks, and then Aunt Betty spoke up, "I don't know that there's anything to it, there's probably not, but Isabella has been seen out with Christian a few times."

Molly's heart sank. Was he back with Isabella already? If that was true, then she had to question if Christian had ever felt the way she had. Apparently not. Her misery must have been apparent on her face, because her mother stood up and gave her a hug.

"We weren't going to say anything, but it has been a few months now, and if Christian is moving on, maybe you should do the same."

"No, I'm glad you told me. Let's change the subject. What should we get on our pizza?" While they debated the various toppings, Molly made up her mind to definitely see Kyle again, and to try and stop thinking about Christian, because it didn't seem as though she was on *his* mind.

Christian couldn't stop thinking about Molly. He thought it would be easier once she was gone and he could get back to living his life the way he'd always done it. But that was impossible. The house seemed emptier than ever, like all the life had been drained out of it. He wasn't sleeping well and he knew he'd been a bear to be around, impatient and quick to snap. Travis had called him on it and he'd admitted that he'd been having a tough time of it. But Travis had little sympathy. The solution was simple to him, but Christian wasn't ready to go there, not yet. He wanted to give Molly time to figure out what she really wanted and to experience the job she'd dreamed about.

Molly had a great visit with her mother and Aunt Betty, and a few days after they left, Kyle called to suggest going to dinner that Saturday night. He picked her up at 7:30 and they went to an interesting Ethiopian restaurant, where there were no utensils and they shared several dishes and used pieces of soft bread to scoop up the fragrant meats and vegetables. Molly was surprised by how much fun she had with Kyle. They laughed at the novelty of eating with their hands and it made for a comfortable, informal feeling. They had plenty to talk about and Molly felt like she was having dinner with an old friend. Which, she realized could be an issue, as what she didn't feel was the crazy excitement and attraction that she'd felt with Christian. But, maybe that was okay. Maybe nice and fun and comfortable could be a good thing too. Maybe the attraction would come after they'd spent more time together, and when she stopped comparing him to Christian.

It was a beautiful clear night, and after they finished eating they decided to walk back to Molly's place instead of getting a cab. When they reached the door of her apartment building, Molly debated whether or not to invite him in, but before she decided, he said, "I have an early meeting in the morning, so am going to grab a cab home. I had a really great time tonight and would love to do it again soon, if you're up for it?" He smiled and Molly didn't hesitate. "I'd love to." She had enjoyed the evening as well, and would be happy to spend more time with him.

"Great, I'll call soon and we'll make a plan." He leaned over, gave her a quick peck on the lips and then was on his way.

Two nights later, Molly was home for the evening and had just climbed into her softest pajamas and curled up on the sofa to watch a little TV, when the phone rang. At first, she guessed it might be Kyle calling to make plans for the coming weekend, but then she saw the caller ID and the butterflies came rushing back: it was Christian's cell phone number.

"Hello?"

"Molly, it's Christian." He sounded uncertain and very far away.

"Hi, what's up?" She tried to sound casual and friendly.

"How've you been?" he asked.

"Good, busy with work. You?"

"Same. Listen I'm calling because I have to come to New York tomorrow and would love to see you, see how you're doing. Are you free to meet up for dinner tomorrow night? I could meet you at Becco's after you get off work, or anywhere else you want to go?"

"Becco's is fine. I should be able to get there by 6:30. Why are you coming to New York?" she asked.

"A business meeting. I'll tell you more about it when I see you."

"Okay," she agreed. "See you tomorrow night."

"Looking forward to it." His voice sounded more confident now, more like the Christian she used to know.

Molly was a bundle of nerves the following day. She was so distracted that she kept forgetting what she was about to do, and had to check her to- do list repeatedly to make sure she stayed on track. Finally, she was able to wrap up for the day and jumped in a cab to go to Becco's.

Christian was waiting for her outside the main entrance and pulled her into a hug as soon as she reached him.

"Have you been waiting long?" she asked him.

"No, just got her a minute before you did. Are you ready to head in?"

He held the door for her, and they went inside and were seated immediately. The waiter came and they ordered a bottle of Amarone, a smooth red that went wonderfully with the pasta. Christian ordered a sirloin steak and Molly got what she always got at Becco's: the triple pasta. The pastas changed daily, but they were always delicious. Tonight was light-as-air gnocchi in a gorgonzola cream sauce with walnuts, rigatoni with spinach and scallops and fettucini with a light tomato and onion sauce.

As they drank their wine and ate their meals, they caught up on everyone they knew and what everyone was up to.

"How's the job going? Is it everything you'd hoped?" Christian asked.

"It's fine. It's going well. Everything is wonderful," she said with forced enthusiasm.

"I heard that you're dating." Christian stated. Molly thought that was interesting. The only people who knew about Kyle were her mother and her aunt, and she knew her mother would never say anything. What was Aunt Betty up too?

"I've gone on a couple of dates. Kyle is a nice guy." She couldn't help adding, "I think you'd like him." He glowered at that, and then Molly asked,

"I heard you and Isabella are back together?"

Christian looked outraged at the thought. "What? Where did you hear that?"

"You were seen out with her a few times. People assume things."

"Well, they would be assuming wrong. We are most definitely not back together. We were meeting to discuss a possible business deal."

"What kind of business would you have with Isabella?"

"She wants to unload her inn. It turns out she's not meant to run a B & B." He smiled at that. "She wanted to ask my advice and if we might be interested in taking it over. I told her I'd run the idea by you, but that I didn't know if you'd have any interest in another Montana property."

"That's the business meeting you referred to? With me?" Molly was a little confused. "You could have just called."

"No, I couldn't. I needed to see you, to look you in the eyes and see if you're happy here. Or if you might ever be happy somewhere else, say in Beauville maybe?"

Molly's heart raced. "What are you asking exactly?"

Christian smiled then, and Molly caught her breath at the sight of the laugh lines that danced around his mouth and the cute little crinkles around his eyes when he grinned. He dropped to one knee and took Molly's hand. "Molly I love you, and I've been missing you like crazy. Would you consider staying married to me?"

"Seriously? Yes, of course! What took you so long?"

He kissed her then, a long kiss that resulted in the tables around them clapping. He sat back down and took her hand again.

"It's been hell, this waiting. I wanted to give you enough time to feel like you'd really tried out the new job and that you weren't giving something up to be with me. I was going to wait another month or two to be sure, but then when I heard you'd met someone, I panicked. I couldn't risk losing you."

"You wouldn't have lost me. Kyle's a sweetheart, but he's not you."

"So, what do you think about Isabella's idea? If you took over her place, you'd have plenty to do between that and Rose Cottage." Molly loved the idea and now that she had Ann already working as a manager, it would be a simple transition.

"I love the idea, and more importantly, I love you. You have no idea how much I've missed you."

"I think we owe a toast to Gramps," Christian said. "If it hadn't been for him, we probably wouldn't be together."

"To Gramps!" Molly agreed, and then clinked her glass against Christian's. "And to the rest of our lives, together." She leaned over then and kissed him, and then they started making plans. As soon as she could work out her notice, she'd be on her way home to Montana and back to her husband...

~The End~

If you enjoyed SIX MONTHS IN MONTANA, and want to be the first to know when MISTLETOE IN MONTANA is available, (Dan and Traci's story), please sign up for my New Release Alerts. I hate spam and will never share your email or bother you. I'll just send the occasional note to let you know when new releases are available, special promo prices, cover reveals & giveaways. Thank you! http://eepurl.com/IZbOH

Also coming soon is TRUST, my cozy mystery. As it's getting closer to an actual release date for TRUST (shooting for mid-end of December), I thought I'd post a little teaser. The prologue is set twenty years before the story begins....thanks for reading!

How well do you really know your significant other? If they were accused of a crime would you trust in their innocence unconditionally? That's the premise of TRUST, where 30 somethings Lauren and David are about to get married, until one of Lauren's students goes missing and she becomes a person of interest.

Prologue

Twenty years earlier . . .

Melissa Hopkins wanted more than anything to be home in her warm bed, securely tucked under her thick down comforter. Instead, for what seemed like an eternity, she'd been sitting in a small, windowless room at the local police headquarters, being interrogated non-stop. It made her head ache, although she supposed the drinks she'd had earlier could be a contributor to that as well. Most of her friends had started drinking a few years ago, around age 14. It was common in Waverly, a beachfront community that was busy in the summer and deadly deserted in the winter months. Her friends considered her a lightweight as she had always said no, until a few months ago on her sixteenth birthday. Melissa closed her eyes and tried yet again to focus, and to remember what really happened, but her memory was a confusing blur. She suspected that she may have blacked out for a bit. That had happened once before when she'd been drinking vodka, and this time they had been playing quarters on the beach and doing shots. Her stomach did an unhappy flip just thinking about it.

"Melissa, your Mom is waiting outside to take you home. As soon as you tell us what we need to hear, you'll be on your way. You want to go home Melissa, don't you?"

The policemen seemed to taunt her. One was a tough Irish looking guy who looked to be in his mid-thirties and was clearly frustrated. The other cop was younger and equally irritated. They started in again, saying the things they'd already said to her, but this time she was hearing them differently. Her mind was too tired to protest.

"Melissa, the other two boys saw you run after Nancy with the murder weapon. Your prints are all over it, along with her blood. You were mad at Nancy, you admitted that already. You obviously did this Melissa."

Her head started to throb and she pressed a hand against her forehead, willing the pain to go away. "They saw me run after Nancy? Holding something?" It was so hard to focus.

"Yes, Melissa. Just admit you killed her, all the evidence makes it very clear. If you confess, things will go much easier for you. We don't think you meant to do this. You didn't mean to kill her, right Melissa?"

"No, I didn't mean to kill her." Melissa felt bewildered, like she was being pulled underwater or in some kind of surreal dream.

"Say you killed her and you can go home. We can all go home." Their voices were kinder, and softer and Melissa really, really wanted to go home. She'd lost track of how many hours she'd been in this room, but it was much too long.

"I guess maybe I did it, I'm not really sure. I must have though, right?"

"Yes. Good girl, Melissa. We'll go get your mother."

Don't forget to get on my new release alert list to be notified as soon as TRUST and MISTLETOE IN MONTANA are available! http://eepurl.com/IZbOH

Acknowledgements

Thank you to all of my friends and family who have supported this dream. Fellow writer friends, Marley Gibson, Janet Campbell Cardoso and Dana Finnegan who have been so supportive and encouraging, special thanks to Dana for making sure I got the Bozeman details right.

About the Author

Pamela Kelley lives and works in Plymouth, MA and has always been a huge book worm. She worked as a journalist many years ago and in recent years as a food writer for local papers. She is very excited to finally be following her passion to write the kinds of books she loves to read.

Recipe

Here's the lobster dish that Molly served at the wine dinner. I'm lucky in that I live near the beach and local fresh lobsters are almost always available. The key to this dish is the freshest, sweetest lobster meat. In a pinch, you could use fresh frozen, but only if you're dying for lobster and simply cannot get a hold of the fresh stuff. You could boil your own whole lobsters, but it's so much work, and messy. Easiest way to go is just buy a pound or two of fresh shucked meat. If they're hard to get or too expensive where you live, you can easily substitute your favorite seafood, shrimp, scallops, or any mild white fish also works well. Sometimes I like to mix all three, for a seafood medley!

Lazy Lobster Casserole

1 pound fresh lobster meat, chopped into roughly 1 inch pieces

1 stick of butter

1 sleeve of Ritz crackers

2 tablespoons sherry (optional)

2 tablespoons chopped, fresh, flat parsley

Melt 3/4 stick of butter in a small bowl. In a medium casserole dish, place lobster, and pour half the melted butter over and stir to coat. Add Ritz cracker crumbs and parsley to the remaining melted butter. Mix well, and then pat over top of lobster meat, until evenly coated. Cut remaining butter into small pieces and dot over top of stuffing. Drizzle sherry evenly over the top, and bake for about 25 minutes at 300 degrees.

Serves 3-4

This also makes an excellent side for Surf and Turf. We served it up recently with grilled tenderloins, and had a simple tossed salad with balsamic vinaigrette, toasted walnuts and goat cheese.

Enjoy!

~Pam